(Lg. print)
McInerny, Ralph (Mys.)   AF
The Green Revolution   McI

	DATE DUE		
1615	2-18-11		
1615	2/1/14		

THE GREEN REVOLUTION

 This Large Print Book carries the
Seal of Approval of N.A.V.H.

THE GREEN REVOLUTION

RALPH MCINERNY

THORNDIKE PRESS
A part of Gale, Cengage Learning

GALE
CENGAGE Learning·

Detroit • New York • San Francisco • New Haven, Conn • Waterville, Maine • London

GALE
CENGAGE Learning™

LIBRARY OF CONGRESS CATALOGING-IN-PUBLICATION DATA

McInerny, Ralph M.
    The green revolution / by Ralph McInerny.
      p. cm. — (Thorndike Press large print basic)
    "A mystery set at the University of Notre Dame"—T.p. verso.
    ISBN-13: 978-1-4104-1183-9 (hardcover : alk. paper)
    ISBN-10: 1-4104-1183-4 (hardcover : alk. paper)
    1. Knight, Roger (Fictitious character)—Fiction. 2. College teachers—Fiction. 3. Knight, Philip (Fictitious character)—Fiction. 4. Private investigators—Indiana—South Bend—Fiction. 5. University of Notre Dame—Fiction. 6. South Bend (Ind.)—Fiction. 7. Large type books. 8. College stories. I. Title.
PS3563.A31166G738 2009
813'.54—dc22   2008038995

Published in 2009 by arrangement with St. Martin's Press, LLC.

For Charlie Callahan

In memoriam

PROLOGUE

At the Notre Dame Grotto, which is a replica of the grotto at Lourdes, votive candles cast flickering light on the statue of Mary. Before her kneels St. Bernadette in prayer. On this Saturday evening, she was joined by bands of bewildered fans who had crept down here from the stadium seeking spiritual consolation in their gloom.

"We could have won."

"We *should* have won."

Strange remarks in a sacred place? Prayer is a many-faceted thing — petition, thanksgiving, repentance. Why should sharing one's disappointment with the patroness of Notre Dame after one more loss not find entry on that list?

Many had not laughed when Trooper Tim McCarthy, in the closing minutes of the game, told his awful joke and urged them to drive carefully home. Some were not even in the stadium at that time. Did fellow

9

Christians linger in the Coliseum while their friends were fed like lunch to the lions? Nittany Lions.

The pain that follows the loss of a game in which one's favorite team has played would not, for many, rank high among the sorrows of the Western world. There are always philosophers among us, measuring our joys and griefs on a scale that diminishes both. But philosophers are often wrong. Some of them speak of language as a game — but can you lose it? The grim either/or of an athletic contest, win or lose, is tolerable before the game begins, but who can take comfort from that disjunction when the final whistle has blown and another loss has been recorded? For centuries, men and women have gone on pilgrimage for less, and so these fans have come to the Grotto.

Elsewhere, tailgaters gathered around their vehicles, no remnant of the elation they had felt before the game visible. Some of the kids — ah, the resilience of youth! — were passing a football back and forth. The football is an oddly shaped object, meant to travel in a spiral when thrown. A ball tumbled through the air, end over end, and was caught. A cheer went up. The mourning adults looked sadly at their offspring.

The parking lots began to empty; tens of

thousands of cars were expertly directed by the local constabulary and sent on their way. In a few hours most would be gone, back to Chicago, to Detroit, to all points on the compass. When they reached the toll road, they could look back and see, in the waning light of the day, the great statue atop the golden dome, Mary standing tall and unbowed, looking south. It might have been the direction in which the team had been headed since the beginning of the season.

In Holy Cross House, the residence of retired members of the Congregation that had founded Notre Dame, an old priest read his breviary. "How long, O Lord, how long?" He might have taken it as the psalmist's desire for refuge. He might have taken it more personally, as a reference to his own approaching death. His eyes lifted from his book to look across the lake at the now illuminated golden dome. He sighed.

Yet another loss.

How long, O Lord, how long?

PART ONE

1

The 2007 season began with a loss, never a good sign, but what prophet or pundit could have predicted what lay ahead for Notre Dame? Mark May of ESPN excepted, of course, but then a constant Cassandra, like a stopped watch, is bound to be right once in a while. Student sportswriters on the various campus publications ranked the initial performance of the team and found it wanting, yet all were ready to accept and expand upon the excuses that emanated from the athletic department. This was a young team. Too many starters from the previous year were gone. Brady Quinn was gone. Three different quarterbacks were tried in the first game! Not to worry, once that problem was settled and a starter chosen, things would fall into place. Well into the consecutive losses, these loyal sportswriters were predicting Notre Dame victories in the next contest.

Hope is a fragile thing, trust less so, but the two become linked in the minds of football fans. As the losses mounted, at home and away, every game televised nationally, thus giving the collapse of the Notre Dame program maximum coverage, criticism began. The first demand that Charlie Weis must go appeared in the letters column of the *Observer.* Surely a band of loyal and affluent alumni could be found to buy out Weis's contract and bring in someone who would restore the fortunes of the storied team.

Already, summer soldiers in the stadium had expressed their discontent with a play, a halted drive, a missed tackle, sometimes in other than colorful language. This was standard fare, and these were fans whose emotions swung easily from elation to gloom even in the best of seasons. Criticism from students expressed days after a game when presumably reason had reestablished itself suggested a more serious problem. The appeal to the alumni had not attracted the millions necessary to buy out the coach's contract, but it did elicit rumblings from the far-flung Notre Dame family.

It would be difficult to explain to someone from another planet or even another country the role that football plays at the University of Notre Dame. Once incoming freshman had been shown *Knute Rockne, All-American,* starring Ronald Reagan and Pat O'Brien, to orient them. More recently, *Rudy* improbably served the purpose of instilling in incoming students, should they need it, an understanding of the mystical significance of Notre Dame football. During their four-year stay, most will respond to this message. The student section in the northwest curve of the stadium, recognizable by the identical T-shirts worn, is always full, and the students stand throughout the game. Win or lose, after the game the team comes to stand before this section, helmets aloft, to salute their fellow students and thank them for their support.

When these young men and women go out into the world as alumni they do not, as the graduates of other colleges may, lose touch with the Saturday doings on fall afternoons in South Bend. A contract with a national television network ensures that every game will be brought to them wherever they may be. Often they gather under the auspices of the local alumni club and renew that sense of mystic solidarity that was theirs when as students they followed the game inside the stadium. Indeed, the sense of solidarity with the university and the team — a distinction without a difference in the minds of many — increases as graduates age away from their days on campus. Even those few who had been less than enthusiastic fans of the team as students find the true faith entering them in later years. There are homes from coast to coast, otherwise indistinguishable from others in the neighborhood, that are gripped in gloom in the days after a Notre Dame loss. And, it must be said, there are triumphalist alumni who stud their lawns with leprechauns, fly green pennants from the corners of their garages, and sometimes even rush into the street to shout and cheer, doubtless to the mixed reactions of the Purdue and Michigan and Southern California alumni in the neighborhood. These enthusiastic souls would be put to a grim moral test during the historic 2007 season. Many did not pass it.

The symbiotic connection between the American college and football goes back into the dim past of the nation. Institutions of learning, most of them founded under religious auspices, accepted the ancient maxim of *mens sana in corpore sano.* Games, unorganized at first, were encouraged on those modest campuses of yore.

Our prestigious institutions of higher learning all had modest origins: sectarian, local, their faculties far from the stellar quality that many later would achieve. The rivalries between them were seldom of an intellectual sort; rather, they were sectarian, regional, even social. The members of the Ivy League grew from unprepossessing seedlings, and the games played on their campuses evolved from intramural exercises to contests with rivals; the annual games with Yale or Harvard or Princeton slowly became legendary. Universities founded later mimicked this tradition, and then, one fateful day, hitherto unnoticed Notre Dame beat the invincible West Point team and the Fighting Irish became a national phenomenon.

The Catholics of the country, particularly Irish Catholics, saw the team as their champion in a WASP world, a mode of upward mobility. The subway alumni, more passionately partisan than those who had actually attended Notre Dame, were born. The schools of the Big Ten and then other regional conferences arose and soon eclipsed the Ivy League. Athletic activities were no longer more or less happenstance manifestations of school spirit but the planned and public manifestations of these institutions. Professional football, at first a poor cousin of college leagues, began a steady climb to prominence that was sealed by the advent of television. Once-local clubs, like that sponsored by the packing industry in Green Bay, outgrew their modest beginnings. Professional football was soon big business, with profound consequences for the college game.

College athletes became a recruiting pool for professional football, and the once self-contained campus activity, a four-year involvement sufficient unto itself, came to point beyond, to a career, eventually to a very lucrative career. It was here that a divide occurred. Under this new dispensation, the teams of the Ivy League faded from importance. It was seldom that student athletes from these schools sought or were sought by the prospering members of professional football leagues. In those historic institutions, the game was played as before, with little or no interest in a continuation of the activity after graduation. The storied rivalries among them continued but took on the quaint air of the superseded. Some, like the University of Chicago, abandoned organized athletics entirely and withdrew from competition. The surprising suggestion was made that colleges and universities were chiefly aimed at the acquisition of knowledge and culture. Academic excellence became a watchword. Elsewhere, it was different.

Two truths, once held in precarious balance, came to seem almost contradictory. On the one hand, the aim of a game is to win; on the other, a salutary reminder, a game is only a game. On some historic campuses the latter truth prevailed, on most the former, and these began to professionalize their athletic programs. Coaches were no longer, as in the long ago, simply plucked from the faculty, as Knute Rockne had been taken from the chemistry department; now there were national and public searches for coaches who could ensure a winning program. Television upped the ante. There was money, lots of money, to be had from college football. The bowl games, a story in themselves, became paramount, brooding over the regular season like its ultimate end, a promise of millions more as the old year turned into the new. The professionalization of college football was in fact a fact.

If there was a feverish recruiting of coaches, there was an equally feverish search for athletes who had made names for themselves on the high school level. A chasm grew between students and the athletes that represented an institution on the gridiron. On the campuses of many state universities, student athletes were sequestered into special dorms and offered classes that made few demands on their minds and presented little competition with their primary purpose, winning games. There emerged at places known as football factories the fact, dismaying to some, that a large, even a very large, percentage of athletes failed to graduate despite the easy academic paths that had been devised for them. Since only a small number of them were drafted by professional teams, many young men found themselves with neither a college degree, no matter how undemanding, nor the future of which they had dreamed: playing on Sundays.

On the South Bend campus there was an uneasy ambivalence. On the one hand, under Father Hesburgh, the drive for academic excellence strengthened. On the other, there was a continuing demand for a winning team. Compromises were made. Recruits were brought in from all points of the compass primarily on the basis of athletic ability, but there was resistance to the idea that special undemanding courses should be provided to them. For a time, the notion of student athlete was not an oxymoron at Notre Dame. True, an effective tutorial system for athletes was devised, but this was to help them weather the same courses taken by the rest of the students. Comparatively stringent standards of admission were retained despite the fact that many athletes had come to Notre Dame only as to a good springboard into the ranks of professional athletics. The situation was volatile. The administration sent out, in the phrase, confusing and incompatible signals.

There was continuing emphasis on academic excellence, but this did not diminish the desire for performance on the football field. There were dark days when a coach failed to fulfill expectations, but even the unlucky Gerry Faust had been retained throughout his contract despite a disappointing record. With the firing of Ty Willingham before his contract ran out, a Rubicon was crossed. This firing was difficult to explain. Notre Dame's first black coach, Willingham had a good if not outstanding record. But he lost bowl games, and he was said to be deficient in recruiting players, although he had brought in Brady Quinn and other greats who would haunt the memories of the fans of 2007. It seemed that he and his teams were not professional enough. He was unceremoniously sacked just before Christmas in the third year of a five-year contract. Like another December date, it was for many a day that would live in infamy.

The search for his successor verged on the comic. The new president flew to Utah and was televised by a hovering news helicopter on his pilgrimage to hire Coach Meyer. It emerged that Meyer had already been hired away by Florida. The spectacle of the president of Notre Dame apparently making the hiring of a winning football coach the top item on his agenda marked a historic first. The balance between academics and athletics had been symbolized by the fact that the president of the university kept aloof from hiring coaches. Now the line had been crossed, and with demeaning results. Damage control was called for.

This was the context in which Charlie Weis was brought to Notre Dame from the New England Patriots, where he had been a phenomenally successful assistant coach. A Notre Dame alumnus who had never played football, Weis was offered two million dollars a year to return to his alma mater and get Notre Dame football back on track. His first year bore out those hopes, but he, too, lost a bowl game. The second year was perhaps not as satisfying to the hopes of his employers. Then came his third season, 2007. All Willingham's recruits were now out of the picture; Weis was regarded as a legendary recruiter. The debacle of 2007 was accomplished by players of his choice.

2

In the apartment of Roger and Philip Knight, just to the east of campus, the fortunes of the football team had ever been a matter of eager interest on the part of Philip since their arrival at Notre Dame. Roger, the enormous Huneker Professor of Catholic Studies, sympathized with his brother's enthusiasm, and from time to time even attended a game himself, despite the daunting logistics of getting his three hundred pounds to the stadium and settled on a seat designed for fans of considerably less avoirdupois, but his interest in athletics remained theoretical and remote. It had been only on the eve of completing his doctorate at Princeton that he had come to understand the feverish activity on campus and in town on certain autumn Saturdays. But it was less the commotion surrounding him than an essay of F. Scott Fitzgerald in *The Crack-Up* that had made him aware of

Princeton football.

Scarcely more than twenty years old when he had been dubbed a doctor of philosophy — in philosophy — he had long failed to find an academic berth because of his massive size and eccentric personality and then became almost inadvertently a partner in Philip's private investigation firm. During all those years his involvement in the fortunes of college football had been merely a matter of paying intermittent attention to Philip, who gave running comments on televised games and listened to the endless chatter about them by experts before, during, and after the contest. Engrossed in a book or busy at his computer, keeping up his contacts around the globe with correspondents sharing one or more of his many interests, Roger experienced the crescendo and decrescendo from the television room as merely a pleasant background noise. Then he had been offered a job at Notre Dame.

It would be too much to say that it was Philip who had accepted the offer, but his enthusiasm at the possibility of relocating in South Bend, with the prospect of all those teams to watch close up — his uncontrolled delight, in fact — would have been sufficient to overcome Roger's own predilection for inertia. The offer had been made on the basis of Roger's monograph on Baron Corvo, a legendary nineteenth-century convert, pervert, novelist, and eventual Venetian gondolier who continues to fascinate many. Roger would be an endowed distinguished professor floating free of any departmental involvement; he could teach what the spirit moved him to teach. His intention was to acquaint his students with forgotten elements of Catholic culture, writers, poets, architects, anything but musicians, the latter precluded by his tin ear.

In the fall of 2007, he was offering a course on Catholic involvement in the revival of interest in the liberal arts, and the concomitant rise of interest in the great books of the Western tradition, that had taken place in the 1930s. In this he was aided greatly by having as his friend Otto Bird, the founder of what was now called the Program of Liberal Studies. Otto had known personally many of the pivotal figures in that revival, and he had worked with Mortimer Adler at the *Encyclopedia Britannica,* editing the *Great Books of the Western World* in each volume of which he himself published a lengthy, impressive essay on one of those great books. To Roger's wondrous delight, two of those essays had been thorough yet compact studies of Aquinas's *Summa theologiae* and Dante's *Divina Commedia.* As it happened, Otto was visiting Roger when the 2007 season began its slow descent.

There were philosophical fans who could take comfort in the adage that you win some, you lose some. Philip Knight was not among them. There were fans who attributed misfortune on the field to biased officials, probably in the pay of the National Council of Churches. Philip was not among them either, although he sometimes sympathized with the sentiment. The group that included Philip looked beyond an undeniable defeat to the golden prospects of the next weekend when all would be made right, much as, until the eighth race is run, losing gamblers summon hope and throw good money after bad. It was precisely this eternally rising hope that proved to be all too temporary as the tragic season unfolded. And soon would come the games that even pessimists expected the Irish to win.

The sardonic billed it as the battle of the titans. Navy had not beaten Notre Dame since the days of the immortal Roger Staubach. Their 2007 season equaled that of Notre Dame in pathos, though less had been expected of the team from Annapolis.

The bruised and battered Notre Dame fan felt, not without reason, that here at last, however equivocally and against a lesser opponent, something like redemption must come. Not even the prescient could have known that when the four regular quarters of the games had been played out the two teams would find themselves tied. Not even Cassandra could have foreseen that the Navy game would go into overtime. Into three overtimes, in the last of which Navy would score and hope would finally die in Philip's breast and in those of many others.

But all that lay in the future.

Otto and Roger were in the study leafing through an ancient folio volume, a product of the first generation of printing, the commentary of Thomas Aquinas on all the epistles of St. Paul. Otto was now in his nineties, his health not good but his mind clear and his zeal for learning unchanged. He was disposing of his considerable and valuable library.

"I want you to have this," he had just said to Roger.

"If only I could afford it."

"I meant as a gift."

Roger's astonishment was as great as Philip's when he burst into the apartment, returning from the stadium where Notre

Dame had just lost to Southern Cal, though that of one brother was the astonishment of pleasure, that of the other the astonishment of the betrayed.

"We lost!"

Otto Bird, one of the great figures on the Notre Dame faculty during the past half century, always impeccably dressed, easily one of the most learned men Roger had ever known, looked at Philip in surprise.

"We lost again!" Philip's voice had dropped to a horrified whisper, his expression that of the devout when they repeat a heretical phrase.

"What was the score?" Roger asked, his pudgy hand moving reverently over a page of the volume he had just acquired, feeling the imprint the letters had made centuries ago on the paper.

"We should have won!"

Otto's interest in the athletic fortunes of the university to which he had devoted a long lifetime was, not to put too fine a point upon it, minimal, but he had become accustomed to outbursts such as Philip's over the years. He had found that sympathetic silence was the best response, a silence that could be interpreted as acquiescence in the burden of the outburst. His benign expression had not altered on autumn Mondays

31

when all around him in the faculty lounge each play of the previous Saturday's game was subjected to professorial if not professional analysis. Well, why not? Noncombatants write the history of battles, outwit Napoleon while comfortable at their desks, say yea or nay to Churchill's plan for a second front in World War II, not across the Channel but up through the "soft underbelly of Europe." Wars are more easily waged in retrospect, and games that had been lost on Saturday are turned into possible victories on Monday. Otto did not condescend to such colleagues. After all, what is teaching but a long retrospective conversation about the achievements of others?

It was clear that Roger and his guest were not to be let off easily. A thoroughly disenchanted review of the game followed.

"We could have won it if only . . ."

The sensible course Philip outlined had not been followed by the coaching staff. How could their decisions be attributed to misfortune? Only inepititude on the sidelines could explain such a failure to win the game and winning was the expected ending of every Notre Dame game.

Eventually Phil fell silent, and into the silence Otto introduced the games Aeneas had scheduled for his crew, bringing their ships ashore and letting the contests begin. Afterward, there was a massive feast for the contestants.

"I have often thought," Otto said softly, "that we are unwise to reverse that order. Our feasting and burnt offerings come before the game."

"There will be no feasting and celebrating tonight," Phil said. He rose and wandered off, and Roger and his guest returned to a discussion of the early days of printing, with especial reference to the folio volume that Otto had given Roger as a gift.

When the phone began to ring, Roger did not answer, assuming that Phil would take the call. Many rings sounded before Roger picked up the phone to hear Father Carmody on the line. Father Carmody, a more eminent figure on the campus than even Otto Bird, had been Roger's champion for the Huneker Chair, and since he had connections with the Philadelphia family that was putting up the money, his wishes had overridden those of a faculty committee that had been formed to offer advice on potential occupants of the chair. The name of Roger Knight had not been on their list. It was unlikely that any members of the committee had even heard of the author of the monograph on Baron Corvo. Thus it was that Roger had arrived on campus with a sizable number of unknown enemies who resented his hiring. Meanwhile, Father Carmody had become a friend of the Knight brothers. From time to time, he had also availed himself of Philip's role as private investigator.

"How is Phil taking it?"

"He's upset."

"So were we."

3

In the psalms that Father Carmody read daily, old age was accounted one of God's blessings. For Charles Carmody, it had come to seem a mixed blessing. Throughout his long career in the congregation of Holy Cross, much of it spent on campus, some of it in Rome when he served as right-hand man to the superior general of the order, he had relished the role of the man behind the scenes. Long before his reddish hair turned white, he was known as an Èminence grise, a kingmaker but never a king. And long after his coevals had disappeared from the scene, called to God, or debilitated, drooling denizens of the final station in the life of a member of the Congregation of Holy Cross, Father Carmody remained active, playing a discreet role, advising a series of presidents he had difficulty taking completely seriously. To the old, the young inevitably seem mere parodies of the giants they have succeeded.

Still, when his advice and counsel were asked for they were gladly given. The personnel changed, but the university to which Charles Carmody had devoted himself wholeheartedly remained. The first time he had come along Notre Dame Avenue and seen the great golden dome lift above the trees, he had fallen in love as other men fall in love with mortal women. He became a champion in the service of the Lady atop the dome.

Remaining as active as he had, Carmody had resisted any suggestion that he was ready for Holy Cross House, the low building on the far side of the lake to which retired and ailing and senile members of the congregation went. All very well for them, of course, and thank God there was such a bright efficient place in which they could live out their final days. He knew it was pride that prevented him from seeing himself among the residents of Holy Cross House. Eavesdropping on his inner thoughts, he feared that he heard the voice of the pharisee in the gospel thanking God that he was not like the rest of men. And then one surprising day, without fanfare, Father Hesburgh took up residence in Holy Cross House. Father Hesburgh! If the fabled longtime president of Notre Dame could live in Holy Cross House, who was Charles Carmody to resist? Besides, there was the fact that Hesburgh remained active, on campus and abroad, his demanding schedule seemingly unaltered by retirement from the presidency. Ted's failing eyesight was a handicap few even knew of, but each day he went off to his offices on the thirteenth floor of the library named for him. This seemed the best of both worlds to Charles Carmody, and soon he followed the precedent of Ted Hesburgh and moved into Holy Cross House. For a time, the parallel worked. Like Hesburgh, Carmody continued to be summoned to the main building when matters became too difficult for the youngsters there.

Undeniably, however, there had been a falling off of such summonses of late. There were dark times when Carmody felt that he was on the shelf for good, like the other residents of Holy Cross House. It was more and more difficult to think that he, like Hesburgh, was an exception. He even found himself reviewing his memories with an eye to listing the times when he had pulled the administration's chestnuts from the fire, alone or, recently, in tandem with Philip Knight. It did not help that, surveying the record of the new administration, he felt that they could only benefit from calling on the wisdom and experience of Charles Carmody.

No need to give much thought to how easily he might have spared them the ignominy of pursuing coaches no longer on the market or letting out the astronomical salary that had lured Weis back to his alma mater. Carmody remembered that the most Ara Parseghian had ever been paid as head football coach was thirty-five thousand dollars. Doubtless those who had offered the princely sum to Weis had taken comfort in his early performance. Incredibly, they had extended his contract for ten years after what increasingly looked like a lucky first season. Hubris and folly were to take their lumps in 2007.

Alumni were on the phone to Carmody increasingly as the horrors of 2007 unfolded. Ever the loyalist, Carmody had calmed the angry, encouraged the despondent, appealed to the apparently bottomless love of their alma mater in the graduates of Notre Dame. But in the private forum of his mind he permitted critical judgments to formulate themselves. This was no ordinary string of bad luck. History of the worst kind was being made by the multimillionaire head coach. Of course, Carmody kept such thoughts to himself.

Iggie Willis, an alumnus whose devotion to his alma mater bore some relation to his not undistinguished four years on campus, had been roused to unusual ire by the collapse of the football team. After the first loss, to Georgia Tech, Father Carmody had counseled him to take comfort in the fact that lowly Appalachian State had beaten archrival Michigan. Whatever temporary solace this afforded Willis, it evaporated when Michigan trounced Notre Dame in Ann Arbor. At least the slaughter had not occurred in the very stadium, however altered, that Rockne had built.

"Something has to be done, Father," Willis growled after the loss to Georgia Tech. They were in Leahy's, the bar of the Morris Inn, if not drowning their sorrows then dowsing them with the balm of oblivion. At least Willis was. Carmody, as was his wont, nursed a single drink, all things to all men except in sin.

"It's only a game, Ignatius."

"Life is a game, Father," Willis said in homiletic tones. "A game we're meant to win."

"The stakes are somewhat different."

"Three quarterbacks, Father. Three quarterbacks! What in hell have they been doing during training?"

"Do you know what you get back when you give a dollar for a seventy-five-cent purchase, Willis?"

"You find me a quarterback for that price and I'll buy him."

Father Carmody offered Willis the consolations of philosophy, or the Leahy's equivalent thereof. He recalled with uncanny accuracy past troughs in the record of Notre Dame football. What were a few losses against such memories of redemption?

But the opening loss had been followed by another and another and another . . . Willis began mobilizing fellow enraged alumni; he initiated a Web site and asked fellow Domers to subscribe to the expression of outraged disappointment, which, as the weeks went by, began to seem almost moderate. After the fourth loss, there were more than ten thousand subscribers to Willis's Web site. This development filled Father Carmody with foreboding. The mark, the essence, of a Notre Dame graduate was unquestioning, even blind, allegiance to the great university that had improbably arisen on the shores of St. Mary's and St. Joseph's lakes, the bifurcated bodies of water created from the one lake that figured in the original title of the institution, Notre Dame du Lac. Now on Willis's Web site began to appear what were, let us hope, unserious suggestions that Chicago alumni might know how to arrange for taking out a contract on the now odious coach whose own contract and compensation were subjects of morose delectation. Of such things did alumni chat without inhibition on CheerCheerFor*Old*NotreDame.com, the italicized adjective meant to refer to the golden era before the present debacle.

Not unsurprisingly, Father Carmody eventually got a call from the Main Building. Not from the president. Not from the provost. Not from the inflated platoon of assistant and associate presidents and provosts, not even from Genoux, his one-time protégé who was now special advisor to the president, but from one Kevin Dockery who identified himself as in the foundation and was calling on behalf of the administration.

"And what can I do for you, Mr. Dockery?"

"Are you aware of the Web site CheerCheerFor*Old*NotreDame.com?"

"Tell me about it," Father Carmody suggested, decades of experience counseling the wisdom of indirection.

41

Dockery told him. "They're killing us, Father. Any number of promised donations have been put in escrow until something is done about the football team."

"I am sure the lads are doing their best," Father Carmody said, employing a Leahy's designation for the players.

"It's the coach they're after."

"So what are you doing?"

"The question is, what can we do?"

"Who suggested that you call me?"

This flustered Dockery. Whatever the urgency of his concern — the current drive for contributions, one of a continuous series — it did not emanate from him.

"Perhaps you should have them get in touch with me," Father Carmody suggested and said good-bye to Kevin Dockery with a satisfaction that would become a prominent item in his next examination of conscience.

Within the hour, his phone rang again.

"Father Carmody?"

Ah. Genoux. "Is that you, Neil? How long it's been since we talked."

"You above all know the ceaseless business of administration, Father."

"Ah, but that is all long since, Neil. I find myself increasingly content with the inactivity of this place. The soul, Neil. The soul.

One must prepare himself to meet his maker."

"We need your help, Father."

"Mine?"

How sweet it was to hear the desperation in the voice of the young man, once a protégé, now all but a stranger since he had entered the inner circles.

"You know Ignatius Willis. You can get through to him."

"Oh, I hear from him regularly."

"You do!"

"The loyalty of old students is a touching thing, Neil." The knife being in, he twisted it gently. "Most old students."

Carmody let Genoux cajole and woo him for fifteen minutes before he agreed to do what he could do to get Iggie to call off his assault on Notre Dame football. As it happened, Iggie planned to fly in during the coming week.

"But you'll be too busy for us to get together," Father Carmody had suggested when Iggie called.

"Too busy! Father, I'd cancel appointments to visit with you, and you know it. Besides, I want to give you a report on the Web site."

"What brings you to South Bend? You're not just pretending other business in order to accommodate me."

"Oh, no. There's other business. But that, too, can wait."

4

Father Neil Genoux occupied an office not far from that of the president in the Main Building. His title, special advisor to the president, had a political redolence to it, fittingly enough no doubt. His was the kind of job that Father Carmody had done informally for years and years, through administrations from Cavanaugh's to the present. No title for Carmody, no office either with his name on the door, nor, Genoux was sure, had Carmody been treated so peremptorily by those he served. There were times when Genoux felt like lifting his arms before his chest, curling his hands downward, and barking. There was an old country-western song that had stuck in his memory. *"Take This Job and Shove It."* Or words to that effect. After barking, he would belt out that song and walk out the door, cashiered, reduced to the ranks, free.

Up is down in academe and vice versa.

Malcontents on the faculty regard the administration as the owners, the bosses, and themselves, more improbably still, as working stiffs. They look with resentment on those who wield, as they think, absolute power over them. Power! Those in the administration are the playthings of forces they cannot control, actors in a drama they have not rehearsed, menaced by faculty, alumni, staff, donors, conscience. More and more, Genoux found himself envying the blissful lives of the faculty. Study, teach a few courses a week, loll around chatting with students or colleagues, criticize the administration — lives of total tranquillity. Genoux had taught, he knew better, but his longing swept away realistic memories and he imagined himself back in his office in Decio, chair tipped back, looking out the window, just watching the grass grow. He would never have heard the name of Ignatius Willis then. Or even of the Weeping Willow Society.

If Genoux was at the moment unoccupied, the inactivity was not restful, for it could be broken at any moment and he sent on some mindless task. When he had been asked to take this job, he had been elated. Literally. His chest seemed to balloon at the prospect. The preparatory year followed by

46

the grand and gaudy installation had been a time of honeymoon when all the world seemed to smile benignly on the new administration, despite the faux pas of that trip to Utah. It sometimes seemed to Genoux that he had counseled against going, not flat out, you understand, but indicating by perhaps imperceptible foot-dragging that he . . . Oh, the hell with it. It had been an exciting trip, and the bad publicity died quickly. There seemed to be a lesson there. A lesson they had not learned.

Genoux had taught English in a department that made chaos seem a formal garden, but he had taught against the grain. The nineteenth century was his. He wallowed in Dickens and Thackeray and Trollope, in James and Twain and Howells and a host of lesser figures who were as familiar to him as, well, family. He celebrated rather than debunked; he had had success in eliciting similar responses from his better students. In his present position, he looked back with longing on what seemed those halcyon days. It was like wanting to be living in an idealized nineteenth century. Alas, he had proved all too susceptible to the invitation to come up higher. Higher! He seemed caught in the inverted cone of the Inferno, involved in a long descent to the waiting ice. What a mistake it had been to waste their first year in office on prolonged discussions of the abominable *Vagina Monologues*. On other campuses, the problem had been dealt with summarily. The presidents of Portland and of Providence had reviewed the play and turned thumbs down. Other presidents had followed suit. A brief and outraged response followed, and then silence. By contrast, they had elevated the odious bit of pornography into the major issue of the year. There had been meetings with the faculty where the majority treated with contempt the notion that the play presented any problem whatsoever. This was a university where academic freedom was the watchword, was it not? The meetings with students had been no better. The notion that such careful consideration would endear the administration to the faculty and student body and the great world beyond seemed a bad joke in retrospect. They had actually attended a performance and been pelted with obscenties and condoms. And emerged to say that the matter was still under review!

No wonder a group of alumni, alerted to such strange goings-on, had formed themselves into the Weeping Willow Society, their Web site helpfully citing Psalm 136. In

Latin! *Super flumina Babylonis, illic sedimus et flevimus cum recordaremur Sion. In salicibus in medio eius suspendimus cithara nostra.* Genoux looked it up. "By the rivers of Babylon, there we sat and we wept, when we remembered Sion. On the willows of that land we hung up our harps." Their theory was that, in the matter of that lesbian play, Notre Dame was under assault from nameless secular and neo-pagan forces. The members of the group began to acquaint themselves with other matters on campus, matters of a sort that they found incredible. The Gay and Lesbian Coalition, Gender Studies, other efforts to attack an imaginary homophobia. Papers were leaked to them and appeared on their Web site. Their calm and forceful letters had respectfully asked for an appointment with the president in which he could explain such matters to them, a request that had never been granted.

Their next great concern, after sexual perversity, had been the issue of Catholics on the faculty. Over recent years, the percentage of Catholic professors had dropped precipitously. The Weeping Willow Society got hold of the white paper on the subject that had been prepared and pointed out that the proposed corrective, far from remedying the situation, ensured that the problem would increase. Of course there were members of the faculty who regarded this topic with loathing equal to their hesitation to permit the *Monologues* to be put on under university auspices. They professed to feel menaced. They saw this concern as retrogression, an attempt to reverse the great strides Notre Dame had made in recent years, the restoration of a Catholic ghetto, turned in on itself, hankering for the Inquisition. How often was poor Galileo invoked in such diatribes.

It was the sense that he was failing in his job of special advisor to the president that had turned his thoughts to Father Carmody. What a mistake it had been, though, to seek to enlist the old priest's help through Kevin Dockery. It had made him feel duplicitous when he telephoned Carmody, but the old priest had made no reference to the plea from a surrogate in the foundation. Barring an interruption, Genoux would head for Holy Cross House within the hour.

His first thought when he pulled into the parking lot and saw a man seated just outside the entrance smoking a cigar was that here at least the ban against smoking inside could have been grandfathered.

He approached the old man swiftly, hoping that his agility did not seem an insult.

"Good afternoon," he said brightly.

"Hello, Father."

Genoux stopped. When you have done it unto the least of men, you have done it unto me.

"That smells good."

"Would you like one?" Cigars emerged from the old man's shirt pocket like a Latin American musical instrument.

"No!" He actually stepped back. Imagine returning to the Main Building reeking of cigar smoke.

"I'm Father Genoux." He held out his hand. The old man seemed to be studying his life line before taking it.

"I know."

Genoux looked at him more closely. How old was he? "Were you on the faculty, Father?"

The old man sighed. "I'm used to defective memories, living here."

And slowly, out of the fallen flesh, cheeks stubbled with gray whiskers, the absence of teeth, and sunken still-merry eyes, Genoux composed a portrait of the man as he had been. And recognized him. It was like a moment in the *Commedia* when Dante came upon a fellow Florentine.

"Father Witte?"

"Affectionately known as Nit. I had you

in class."

Genoux pulled up a chair and sat. "Of course. Epistemology."

"I met my class in Moreau."

How quickly it all came back. Witte seated at the desk talking to himself, occasionally scrawling illegibly on the blackboard — which was green; Witte had gotten a lot of mileage out of that — ignoring the men before him, winning argument after argument. Nowadays he would have been mistaken for someone using a cell phone.

"Esse est percipi," Genoux cried out in remembrance.

"To think you would remember a fallacy like that. What do they have you doing now?"

Genoux hesitated. "I'm in the English department." This was technically true.

"This place is going to hell in a handbasket. Do you know anyone in the administration?"

Genoux's heart sank. He stood. "I've come to see Father Carmody."

"I asked him to go straighten those birds out, but nothing's happened yet. Of course, he's not the power he once was."

The sliding door might have been a window. "Punch the numbers into that gizmo on the left." Witte gave him the numbers,

Genoux entered them, and the door slid open. "I'm never sure whether that's meant to keep people out or to keep us in," Witte said. It sounded like a problem in epistemology.

"What a delight to see you, Father," Genoux said as the doors slid open.

"Say a prayer for me, Father."

Genoux raised his hand as if in blessing, and the guillotine of the doors closed behind him. How genuine and simple Witte's request had seemed. Was he ill? The cigar might have been like the famous cigarette before the blindfold is put on the one condemned to die.

"Witte? Sound as a dollar," Carmody said, when the nurse at the great arc of a reception desk had directed Genoux down the hall. Carmody's room might have been anywhere, huge, lots of books, a desk that suggested an active life, overlooking the lake. There was the smell of tobacco in the air. Perhaps Carmody had given himself an exemption from the campuswide ban. "Once Witte went back to smoking, all his ailments left him."

"Ho ho."

"Believe it or not."

"Tell it to the surgeon general."

"So what's on your mind? Iggie Willis?"

Genoux sat on a footstool, almost welcoming the symbolism. I will make thine enemy a footstool for thy feet. Then, too, he had come to sit at Carmody's feet. "I would like to see if you couldn't get him to stop stirring up the alumni."

"I thought you would welcome that as a diversion."

"Then you know of the Weeping Willows?"

"Of course. They've consulted me."

"You're advising them!" My God, with Carmody behind them they would soon know all the skeletons in the closet.

"Hardly that, Father. Nor do they need my advice. Surely you realize they are among our most distinguished alumni."

This surprised Genoux. He did not know that. In the past few years his notion of distinguished alumni was members of the board, donors, a few politicians who, alas, were following the lead of other Catholic politicians. Carmody was rattling off names, followed by a brief description. Medal of Honor, Presidential Medal — "Like Ted's" — chief justice of a state supreme court, two novelists, one of whom had won the Pulitzer — "When it meant something" — several auxiliary bishops, a recently named cardinal. Genoux knew of the latter. He had

54

found himself too busy to come to campus to be honored by his alma mater. Genoux realized that he had lumped the founders of the Weeping Willow Society with Willis's Web site.

"I see what you mean."

"If I were still advising . . ."

"Father, that is why I'm here."

"Answer their letters."

"I wish it were that simple."

"Don't they listen to you over there?"

Genoux tried to explain. Everything the Weeping Willows wished to discuss they already knew of with alarming accuracy.

"Someone is leaking information."

Carmody shook his head even as he shook a cigarette from the package he had picked up from the table beside him.

"Maybe the white paper. One of the silliest documents I ever read. Cardinal Newman responsible for the secularization of Catholic universities!"

"How did you get hold of it?"

"The Weeping Willow people brought it to me. They were certain it was a hoax."

"But where did they get hold of it?"

"Do you really think that's the problem?"

Carmody lit his cigarette and dragged on it with relish, eyes closed. A moment later, great clouds of smoke issued from his mouth and nose. Genoux felt he was in a time warp, Witte with his cigar, Carmody with his cigarettes. Carmody noticed his reaction.

"They can't very well tell Ted not to smoke. He opened the way for the rest of us."

Any thought Genoux had had of snitching when he went back to the Main Building fled like Carmody's exhaled smoke. He hadn't come over here as fire inspector anyway. He began to explain the problem, from the viewpoint of the administration. In any conversation, all the documentation the group had gathered would have to be acknowledged as genuine.

"They already know that. They want to know what you're going to do about those things."

Do? It was all the undoing that would have to be done that was the problem, decades of trimming decisions, dancing away from the Catholic character of the place, Oh, not in statements, of course, but in the way things had been done. Carmody saw the problem.

"You have to start unraveling it, Father."

"Can you imagine the publicity?"

"Easily. You would be pilloried, on campus and off. People would begin to think we mean it when we say that Notre Dame is a Catholic university where things that go on elsewhere are simply out of place."

Genoux looked bleakly out the window, across the lake at the golden dome glittering in the sunlight, at the great statue of Mary atop it. What other advice had he imagined Carmody would give him? Hang tough, ignore the faculty and press, keep talking about the Catholic character of the university?

"Father Witte says we're going to hell in a handbasket."

"He's thought that for years. He blames me, at least in part."

"That's not fair." Genoux might have been defending himself.

"Accurate criticism always seems unfair."

On his way back to his special parking place in the shadow of the Main Building, Genoux found himself envying the men whose lives had brought them at last to the peaceful redoubt of Holy Cross House. He wished he were as old as he felt.

5

Professor Guido Senzamacula, despite his name, was professor of French, his speciality Paul Claudel and other figures of the French Catholic renaissance of the early twentieth century. He had been born in Sicily, on the southern coast, a few miles from the birthplace of Pirandello, whose writings he found at once fascinating and perverse. Anti-art, at least the plays. He loved the *novelle* since they evoked his native province and its dialect. His degree was from the Sorbonne, and he had begun his teaching career in Rome, where he had met Father Carmody, whose tales of Notre Dame had fascinated him. He'd had the priest repeat the salaries paid professors several times, incredulous. The first years on campus, when winter came, made Senzamacula think he had made a terrible mistake. He had taught Italian as well as French then, before the department became specialized. At that time, he had no courses in Italian literature; few students advanced far enough for that. He had long since been relieved of the drudgery of teaching grammar, that task given to a host of part-time people with odd titles — assistant academic specialist, and other strings of nouns that defied the tree of Porphyry — doing piecework that kept them off the princely payroll.

Senzamacula was a respected if not beloved professor, jumpier as he got older, despite his idyllic schedule. He had married an American of Swedish extraction, captivated by her honey-blond hair and large blue eyes — and other parts of her, too, of course. Jessica. She had borne him two sons, and she herself now lay in Cedar Grove cemetery. She had died two decades ago, at the age of forty-nine, her once robust body reduced to skin and bones. Guido still dreamed of her, was sometimes wakened by the sound of her voice. Several times a week he stood weeping at her grave and almost longed to lie once more beside her, half in love with easeful death.

There had been several bad spells after Jessica's death, crying jags he could not stop and that had gone on for days. He felt guilty, he felt there was something he might have done, should have done, that he had not done and if he had Jessica would still be alive. "You're Guido, not God," Father Carmody said to him. "Stop this self-pity." Stern words to a grieving man, but they hadn't helped. When he did get back into his routine he felt like a fragile package. He noticed that others treated him with gingerly deference, as if he might break down at any minute.

Olaf, their eldest, had been born retarded, a severe case of Down syndrome. He had died a few years after his mother, and now they lay together in Cedar Grove. That left Piero, whom he saw seldom, except in the fall when his son came with the network he worked for in order to televise Notre Dame football. This brought Piero to South Bend often enough during the season, for every home game, and of late he had sadly shaken his head and said he just couldn't believe it.

"With the Patriots he was a genius."

Guido waited. He had no idea what his son was talking about. It emerged that the Notre Dame football team was recording a historic series of losses. Piero predicted that the coach could not survive such a debacle. Of course, Piero was a graduate of Notre Dame and had always been passionately interested in football. Once long ago, Guido had attended a game. He would never forget the sight of huge heavily padded young men, lined up facing one another, and then suddenly crashing into the opposite line. While this was going on, someone ran with the ball, or it was thrown and sometimes caught. The point of the game seemed to be to maim the opponent, slamming him to the ground, tackling with the intent to cripple. Guido had expected to see lightly clad men kicking a ball up and down the field. How could they call this football? The players actually handled the oddly shaped ball. All around him, spectators were delirious at what was going on on the field. At halftime, Guido had left the stadium and walked back to his house on Angela Boulevard. What game would not seem inane to one who did not understand it? Roger Knight had not been shocked by these heretical statements when Guido told him of his single visit to the stadium.

"I remember the first time I watched a cricket match." It was not a reference to entomology. Whatever Roger's mystification on that first occasion, he had come to understand cricket thoroughly. "Not that I recommend it. Tell me, what do you know of Claudel's illegitimate daughter?"

"A fascinating story. You know *Le partage du midi,* of course. The play is based on his affair with a married woman in China, where he was French consul. She became pregnant, then met up with another lover and went off with him. Claudel himself married and had a family, but throughout the years he continued discreetly to care for the woman and her child."

"Then it's true."

Roger had come upon a book by the natural daughter's daughter — Claudel's grandaughter, in effect. So much for Guido's thought that he was telling his young friend things he did not already know. Until he mentioned his colleague Lipschutz and his notion that the series of losses by the football team was providential.

"In what way?" Roger asked.

"The university now has a perfect excuse to discontinue football."

"I don't think it will come to that."

"Lipschutz thinks all the administration needs is prodding. His weapon, as he calls it, is all this chatter about our being a great research university. Who can take us seriously when the name Notre Dame is synonymous with football? I am quoting him."

"The University of Chicago once had a team. A very good team."

"That is his precedent! Doesn't the administration like to refer to Chicago as a peer institution?" Guido paused. "Bah." He scrubbed the air before him as if it were a blackboard "I did not come here to talk about football."

The advent of Roger Knight a few years before had been, Guido now realized, one of the brightest points in his own career at Notre Dame. He had had many compatible colleagues, and there were others with whom he had been able to discuss his chief interests, but none had approached the profound affinity he felt with the enormous Huneker Professor of Catholic Studies. On their first meeting, Roger had told Guido all about Baron Corvo.

"He died in Venice."

"See Venice and die."

"Is that an Italian expression?"

"A Venetian expression." Guido likened it to the self-congratulating plaque on the entrance gate of Amalfi.

Roger's brother, Philip, was the antithesis of the corpulent font of lore and wisdom. Like Piero, he was depressed by the current football season. For Philip, Guido's main claim to fame was that his son was a member of a crew that televised football games, Notre Dame's among them.

"What does your son make of our season?"

"He thinks the coach will be fired."

It was clear that Phil's discontent did not extend to that. Even Roger was surprised at Guido's reaction to Lipschutz's planned agitation.

"I'm told that there have been rumors like that in the past."

Guido remarked on his own initial surprise at the prominence of athletics on American campuses. "In Italy, the teams are municipal or regional."

Roger feared that Phil might make a wounding comment on taking Italy as precedent. "You're thinking of professional sports, Professor."

Professional? Perhaps college players were not paid, but Piero had mentioned the salary of the Notre Dame coach. Guido had been shocked. When Phil left them, Guido whispered what Piero had told him.

"I think it's even more now. And there are other compensations as well."

"But that is obscene, Roger."

"You might very well think so."

Guido did think so. He found his sentiments moving closer to those of the soon to be crusading Lipschutz.

6

At the Old Bastards table in the University Club, a building scheduled to be demolished by fiat of the administration, the fortunes, or misfortunes, of the football team seemed a clear case of divine retribution.

Horvath said, "Maybe they'll tear down the stadium next."

"The way things are going, the fans may do just that."

Armitage Shanks regarded his tablemates with customary hauteur. Deep in his heart, he found it demeaning to be having his last lunches with such companions as these. The recipient of several Fulbrights over the decades, each time Shanks had returned to campus from those years abroad he saw it with a colder eye. For all that, the club was his refuge, as it was for the other emeriti huddled over their food, keeping a grip on their glasses, anxious to have eating behind them and the prospect of several more uninterrupted drinks ahead.

"I had not thought death had undone so many." Shanks almost sang the line.

"What the hell does that mean?" Potts wanted to know.

"Which word puzzles you?"

"You puzzle me, Shanks."

"I was merely quoting Eliot."

"Ness?"

"No, Loch."

The pretense of illiteracy was a senile defense. He recognized it in himself.

"We'll lose to Navy," Horvath said in somber tones. "Navy!"

"You're going to the game?"

"I was in the marines."

"Do they have a team?"

"Ask the Japs."

He looked furtively over his shoulder. Even at this table, a haven against the madness of the day, political correctness worked its stifling effects.

"Southern Cal will kill us."

"We're already dead," Bingham said. He added quickly, "I meant the team."

"I had not thought football had undone so many."

"This season will undo Weis."

"Don't bet on it."

"I quit betting when I got married," Bingham said.

"You can't lose all the time."

Across the room at the curiously named Algonquin table, half a dozen former assistant coaches of one sport or another were in animated conversation. Debbie, the hostess, came to them directly from that table.

"What are they talking about?"

"Weis. What else? Before I sit down, does anyone want anything?" Without waiting, she pulled out a chair and sat.

"What do they think?"

"He's a dead duck. They've been comparing the salaries they got with what he gets."

"Divine retribution."

"Oh, they all like Devine."

"Debbie," Armitage Shanks murmured, leaning toward her. "When will we run away and live in sin together?"

"You're incapable of running."

"And of sin, my dear."

"Ha."

"I refer to . . . Well, never mind."

"I never do."

"When will the destruction of this place begin?"

"They keep changing the date. After the football season anyway."

"What will you do, Debbie?"

"Maybe retire."

"You're too young to retire."

"I'm too old to be thrown out of here on my ear, too. Do you realize how long I've worked here?"

"Forever?"

"Almost."

"Will you get severance pay?"

"That sounds like recompense for an amputation," Shanks said.

The attitude of the Old Bastards toward the imminent destruction of the club was mixed. On the one hand, the edict from on high confirmed their sense that they had lived into a strange irrational time. On the other hand, the club, this table, meeting here for lunch, anchored their days, giving a semblance of schedule to their waning years.

"I remember when this place opened."

"It was designed by Montana."

"The 49er?"

"He played here first, you idiot."

"I didn't know he was an architect."

"What will happen to the beer steins?"

In glass cases forming a great wall separating the dining area from the rest of the club was housed a collection of beer steins. The donor had made it a stipulation of his gift that the club should house the steins. The donor was dead, but the Gore grandchildren had protested in vain against this building

being torn down on the whim of an admin-
istrator.

"They should sue."

"For breach of promise?"

"For taking money under false pretenses.
If Gore wanted to give a temporary building, it could have been a tent."

"We'll have to find another place to meet
for lunch."

"All good things come to an end."

"So do all bad things. Anyone know of a
place?"

"They'd love to have you at McDonald's,"
Debbie said, pushing back her chair.

"Is that where you're going to work?"

On her feet now, she took a playful swing
at Armitage Shanks. "Your place or mine,
Romeo?"

Shanks sighed. *"O la vie est triste, trop
triste, incurablement triste, n'est-ce pas?"*

"You got me."

"Would that I had, my dear."

This swing was less playful.

"Another round?"

"Splendid idea."

Those facing in the right direction had
the pleasure of observing Debbie's rhythmic
walk as she left them.

7

Some are born journalists, some become journalists, others have journalism thrust upon them. Thus it was that Bartholomew Hanlon considered his election to the editorship of *Advocata Nostra,* one of several alternative student papers that offered relief from the *Observer* whose pages were filled with wire service stories, a good sports section, and editorials that seem to have been mailed in from elsewhere. He was in his senior year and had loaded up on courses he had not had room for in previous years, but his love was the classics, particularly Latin. That love was fed by a deeper love for the Latin liturgy. With others, he cajoled priests into offering the traditional Latin Mass in one of the hall chapels. They had formed a small schola cantorum to accompany the Mass with Gregorian chant. Bartholomew carried in his briefcase the appropriate volume of the *Liturgia Horarum* and read the office of the day. It seemed a way of testing if he had a vocation.

"Everyone has a vocation," Baxter said, lifting most of his chins.

"Then the race will die out."

" 'Tis a consummation devoutly to be wished. No, I don't mean that. No more apocalyptic phrases. Hope springs eternal."

"Spe salvi facti sumus."

"What's that?"

"The title of the new encyclical."

"Another? I haven't caught up on John Paul II yet."

"There's your vocation."

Baxter should be editor, Hanlon thought, but Baxter, an associate editor, had made the mistake of campaigning for the job. Thus Hanlon, who hadn't been at the meeting, had been voted in on the basis of the thwarted hopes of another. No matter. Baxter continued to be a constant presence in the editorial offices, and he had a sassy style that made for compelling reading. He said so himself. It was Baxter who had written up the Weeping Willow Society. Now they were following up on the question of Catholics on the faculty. And how better than by interviewing professors?

"Do we call them first?"

Baxter gave a jowly shake of his head.

"No, no. We surprise them in their lairs. Like reporters on the street stopping passersby. Or is it passerbys?"

Off Bartholomew had gone to Decio, the office building that accommodated most of the Arts and Letters faculty. He had decided to start with Rimini, a frequent contributor of angry letters to the *Observer*. His principal target was critics of what was happening on campus who appealed to a supposedly saner and better time. Rimini knew better. It was hell in those days. He had been here. Believe me, he urged, things are infinitely better now.

Rimini was bald with large staring eyes. Crouched over his desk, he looked at Walsh over the tops of his glasses.

"Professor Rimini?"

Rimini tucked in his chin. His name was prominently displayed beside his open door.

"I'm from *Advocata Nostra*."

"What is that?"

"A student newspaper."

"The student newspaper is the *Observer*."

"There are several alternative student papers now." He smiled. "In the interests of diversity."

"What do you call yours?"

"*Advocata Nostra*. Our Advocate."

"You in the law school?"

"I'm a senior."

"What do you call your paper again?"

"*Advocata Nostra.*"

"Where's that from?"

"The *Salve Regina.*"

"Geez."

"It's the last thing sung over the grave of a member of the Congregation."

Rimini sat back and gave his chair a push. He pointed to another chair. "Just put those things on the floor." In profile, the huge hearing aid that seemed to plug up his ear was visible. "You've been there for the singing?"

"Several times."

"I'll go to the funeral of the last of them." Having said this, though, his lips spread in a smile, displaying huge very white teeth.

"You've been here a long time."

"My junior colleagues take my pulse every morning. One actually held a mirror to my mouth. They're dying to hire my replacement."

"When do you retire?"

"Never!"

His office did not seem a place anyone would want to cling to tenaciously: a little box of a room, a wall of books, the desk a built-in affair, a computer, a strange concrete ceiling that looked like an egg carton.

At least the window gave on a pretty slice of campus.

"So what's on your mind? Football?"

"Would you like to say something about that?"

"Not for publication."

"Actually, I'd like to ask you about the concern expressed by the administration about the percentage of Catholics on the faculty."

Rimini threw back his head and laughed joylessly.

"Anything for publication?"

"Look, put away your notebook. Let me give you some background. I've been here since just after the glacier went through. I've heard that kind of crap from the beginning. It's all PR, aimed at a certain kind of alumnus or alumna — geez, what a word — graduates, and at donors, too."

"You don't think the concern is genuine?"

"Of course not. Look, this place is still in the grip of the Irish drive for upward mobility. We want to be loved. At least they do. The administration. Look at the places they call our peer institutions. You think anyone at Stanford regards Notre Dame as a peer institution? It's peering, all right, peering through the window of the candy store. It's pitiable, calling this place a Catholic research university. Excellence." He sputtered the word.

"But you say that things are better here now." Bartholomew had brought along a sheaf of Rimini's letters to the *Observer.*

"Things are better. Because of the departmental hiring committees. We've been selecting good candidates for years. Do you think they really cared over there that few of them are Catholic?"

"There's a group of alumni who predict that the percentage of Catholics on the faculty will continue to drop."

"Of course it will."

"That doesn't bother you?"

Rimini rubbed his bald head. "Look, I was here when nearly everyone was Catholic."

"Are you?"

Rimini's eyes narrowed, then again the great false smile. "I don't make a career of it."

"You're in economics."

"For my sins." Rimini's eyes widened. "Now where did that come from? As the twig is bent."

"How many in the economics department are Catholic?"

"Who cares? What has being Catholic got to do with economics?"

"Nothing?"

"Not if you want the department to rank high."

"In one of your letters you say some pretty witty things about this obsession with rankings."

"You want consistency, go talk to a philosopher. Besides, I was talking of football. The coaches are out recruiting kids who rank high on the basis of some national scale. Those rankings are about as reliable as rankings of colleges and universities by *U.S. News & World Report.* Who made them the bureau of standards?"

"If I understand you, you're saying that the percentage of Catholics on the faculty is irrelevant."

"That's what I'm saying."

"How about the student body?"

"Talk to Admissions."

Well, as he said, if you want consistency, talk to a philosopher. Bartholomew switched topics and asked Rimini what he thought of the debacle of Notre Dame football.

"Weis is the first Catholic coach since Holtz. I think Holtz was Catholic. There's something for you to pursue. Catholicism and football. What difference does it make whether or not the coach is Catholic? You could make a case that we have done as well, even better, with non-Catholic coaches."

"Interesting."

"Or the football team. Is the administration concerned with the number of Catholics on the football team? Or Caucasians, for that matter? Don't quote me on that," he said hastily. He meant the remark about Caucasians. "For that matter, how many of the Fighting Irish are Irish?"

Rimini was enjoying himself.

"Look," he said. "The administration is pleased with the high percentage of Catholics in the student body. At least among the undergraduates. So how about the percentage in the group of students who bring in real money?"

"The football team."

"Exactly. It's become a money cow. Millions. Millions! Look at what they're paying Mr. Ineptitude."

"What do you think of Professor Lipschutz's suggestion that the time has come to abandon football?"

"He's crazy. But it's an interesting idea."

"You go to the games?"

Rimini sat upright. "I *played* football. Under Ara. Way under. I got in as often as Rudy."

"You don't mind if I mention that?"

"Why should I? I didn't play without a

helmet, no matter what my enemies say."

"Enemies?"

"Let's not go into that."

What fun Baxter would have with such an interview. But what Bartholomew took back with him to the editorial offices was Rimini's suggestion that the administration's concern about Catholic representation should be applied to football, too, to the coaching staff, to the players. Baxter was delighted with Bartholomew's description of his interview with Rimini.

"I think we should pursue that."

"What?"

"How many of the Fighting Irish are Catholics."

"Or Irish?"

"That, too."

And Bartholomew Hanlon went smiling off to Roger Knight's class.

8

Roger had read Mark Van Doren's *Liberal Education* in a serviceman's paperback edition during his abbreviated hitch in the navy. He was perhaps the only seaman with a Ph.D., not that he mentioned this to anyone. The boot camp at San Diego had been grueling, and Roger managed to keep off the weight that he had shed in order to pass the physical. The academic life seeming to be closed to him, he indulged his romantic fancies. He had enlisted on a whim, having just devoured the Hornblower novels, the lure of the sea having him in its grip. All he saw of the sea was San Diego Bay, which was full of gray naval vessels very unlike the one on which Hornblower had sailed. Roger had never been on shipboard either. After boot camp, he awaited assignment, in vain. Finally, his daily presence in the base library having been noticed, he was assigned as assistant to the librarian, a caustic lady, Miss Riggle, who might have inspired the phrase, common at the time, "She'd be safe in the navy." Miss Riggle had regarded Roger as an intrusion on her domain, but when she saw that all he wanted to do was while away the day reading, she grudgingly accepted him. Among the many books he read during the months remaining to him in his country's service was that of Van Doren.

He went on to read others who had been involved in the revival of the liberal arts in the thirties and forties — Mortimer Adler, Stringfellow Barr, Robert Hutchins — a bold band of brothers who were convinced that American higher education had become a wasteland, the elective system their particular bugbear. On what basis was a student to select courses from the smorgasbord presented to him? Was any and every combination of courses the point of education? If a college did not know what the student might become, and how, what right did it have to exist? Even decades later, these revolutionary ideas, largely ignored, could increase the beat of one's pulse. The critique leveled seemed to fit Roger's own experience, although, he told himself, he had managed to use well the nondirective character of higher education. Princeton, however full of certitudes and opinionated professors, left him pretty much to himself. This might have provided a counterexample to the description of the pleaders for a return to the liberal arts and a planned curriculum, but this was not a thought that bothered Roger.

In his seminar, they were now reading Mortimer Adler's onetime best seller *How to Read a Book,* and Otto Bird sat beside Roger, full of anecdotes of what it had been like to work with Adler.

"Don't the requirements for a major provide direction enough?" Bartholomew Hanlon asked.

"What is your major?" Otto asked.

"I have a double major in philosophy and theology."

"What is the aim of the philosophy requirements?"

And so the discussion was under way. Otto had always taught using the tutorial method, and Roger let his senior colleague guide the discussion. What was demanded of a philosophy major? Bartholomew stressed the required courses in the history of philosophy.

"Meant to acquaint you with the great names in your discipline."

"Yes."

"Descartes, Leibniz, Pascal."

"And many others."

"About whom you read secondhand accounts or listen to a professor tell you about their writings. How many of those books were you required to read?"

"It was a survey course."

"Ah."

Otto made the point gently. Why not just read those great works of philosophy?

"That would take a long time."

"Yes," Otto said sweetly. "A lifetime."

Otto himself had spent his long lifetime doing what he indirectly recommended. Even if one concentrated on the great books, one scarcely began to plumb them during four years on campus. No matter. The process begun, it must continue.

Afterward, Otto invited Roger to lunch at the University Club, and they set off in Roger's golf cart. Otto was greeted with delighted warmth by Debbie, who took his arm and led him to "his" table. "Bob Leader and I used to have lunch here once a week," Otto explained.

"The artist?"

"Did you know him?"

"Unfortunately, no."

Debbie took their beverage order and then

joined them, pulling her chair close to Otto's and casting on him a bewitching smile. Clearly, he was one of her favorites. Otto insisted that she should know his guest.

"I haven't seen you here before."

"The door isn't wide enough."

"You got in today."

"Otto held it open for me."

Debbie didn't know what to make of Roger; of course, that was an old story. He didn't know what to make of her either, but he liked the way she catered to Otto.

Otto's executive martini arrived — he had ordered "a bucket of booze" — and Roger lifted his coffee in response to Otto's raised glass.

"You never drink?"

"Alcohol? No."

"Any reason?"

"I just don't like it."

Otto accepted that, but he told Roger of the late Canon Gabriel's maxim. Never trust a man who doesn't drink.

"Well, you can trust him not to drink."

Otto acknowledged this with a smile. Their food came, and over it Otto discoursed on the book he was reading. "The oddest memoir by Saul Bellow's longtime agent. No sense of language at all. I mean the agent."

"What prompted you to read it?"

"I loved *Herzog*. And *Mr. Sammler's Planet*."

"Which has lately brought a charge of racial prejudice."

"Ah, the ironies of liberalism."

Suddenly a compact man with a trimmed beard and a fierce look stood beside their table. "I must speak with you. Both of you. Lipschutz." He thrust out his hand like a holdup man. "May I join you?"

It seemed a rhetorical question, He took the chair on which Debbie had sat.

"I want to enlist your support for a crusade," Lipschutz announced. "This university has arrived at an historic moment. Our precedent will be the University of Chicago."

"I went to school there," Otto said.

"Did they still play football when you were there?"

"I didn't."

"I mean the university. Did it still have a team?"

"I wasn't aware they ever had one."

"Exactly. They regained their soul, and doubtless you were one of the beneficiaries."

Lipschutz laid out the crusade he was embarked upon. The current collapse of Notre Dame football provided their golden opportunity. Like Augustine, Notre Dame had had to wallow in sin before redemption came. The time had come to follow Chicago's lead and abandon football. Let the intrahall games go on, that was fine with Lipschutz, but all the blather about excellence demanded a consistent policy. What a statement Notre Dame could make if it abandoned varsity football because it intended to take its claim to academic excellence seriously.

"Do you think that is realistic?"

"I think it is idealistic! What do you think?"

"It's an interesting idea."

"Do I have your support?"

Later, when his and Otto's names appeared on the list appended to Lipschutz's proposal, Roger was never sure that either he or Otto had actually signed on to the crusade.

9

Ever since his wife left him, Iggie Willis had been trying to reconcile two warring descriptions of himself. Life on the domestic front, and in the office, too, was undergoing a rocky period, no doubt of that, but nonetheless Ignatius Stephen Willis stood craggy and unbowed above the tumbling tide. Much as he liked that picture of himself, there was something to be said for Miriam's portrait of him, a portrait to which she had given a final flourishing touch in the note he found when he had come home to an empty house three months before. "You are a selfish, thoughtless, pompous little man, and if you were tall enough to see into the mirror, you would know that. Good-bye!"

A low blow, that, but who but a wife could know how touchy he was about his height? Let's face it, he was just below five seven, and that was wearing shoes, slightly elevated shoes. Nonetheless, he had always been attracted to taller women. Miriam hadn't been able to wear heels since they were engaged, at least not when they were together. Even then, she looked down at him and, over the years, looked down at him in several senses. What is more perilous than a credit card bill, especially when scrutinized by a wife with the instincts of a CPA?

"There are some bad charges on this, Ig."

"Let me see."

She had checked the two motel charges and one from a florist she had never heard of. Iggie had shaken his head.

"I'll have Pearl take care of it."

"Pearl?"

"It's one of the things she's very good at. Besides, all it takes is a phone call and off the charges come."

"Then why can't you make the call?"

"What am I paying Pearl for?"

A wiser man would have known better than to send his wife flowers the day after that close call; only an idiot would have used the florist that had caught Miriam's eye on the bill. No, that wasn't fair. Pearl was no idiot. He should have done more than just drop the credit card bill on her desk, point to the check marks and roll his eyes. It was an hour or so later that he'd had the big inspiration to send Miriam flowers.

"Any message?" Pearl had asked, not meeting his eyes — but then she would have had to bend her head to do that.

" 'Just because . . .' "

Pearl wrote it on her little pad and went back to her office. Her legs were great with those high spiked heels. It occurred to him later that Pearl had used that florist with malice aforethought. Well, if she had, the effect had been delayed.

"Who's the tall girl you were having lunch with at Chesterfield's?" Miriam asked some weeks later, not lowering the newspaper when she said it.

"That was no girl, that was Pearl." He hadn't missed a beat. Sometimes he amazed even himself. Old quick-witted Iggie.

"You're being talked about." The paper came down and her eyes drilled into him as if she were the dentist, not he.

"So who told you I had lunch with my secretary?"

"How is Prissy supposed to know this glamorous Amazon is your secretary?"

"Maybe I'll put her in uniform."

"How often does this happen?"

He got up and crossed the room and sat beside her on the couch. "Oh, Miriam, not you. The green-eyed monster?"

She might have been one of his patients, rigid in the chair, awaiting the bad news while he studied the X-rays. But he did manage to get his arm around her shoulders. Even so, it was five minutes before she scrunched down sufficiently for him to kiss her. Right then and there, Iggie resolved that it was all over with Pearl.

Pearl proved surprisingly intractable.

"Pearl, we were seen by a friend of my wife's!"

"Having lunch at Chesterfield's. It could have been worse."

A woman is a ruthless thing when she's got you in her clutches. Iggie had thought that Pearl could handle a little fling without making a federal case of it. The next thing he knew, she was crying. He quickly shut the door of his office. For a moment he wanted to strangle her. What had he ever seen in her? Of course she had a little history, a divorce threatened, but that had seemed a recommendation. She had been around the block a time or two. Just a guess, but he had gathered from what she had said that it was her husband who was talking divorce.

"He's even looked into annulments."

"Then you'd really be free."

Of course, she had misunderstood his meaning, but the result of the misunderstanding had been so torrid he hadn't clarified his remark.

After the two close calls, Iggie was the soul of discretion. They never went back to Chesterfield's, and why rent a motel when Pearl had such a convenient apartment? Looking back on it, reading Miriam's farewell address, he couldn't believe how stupid he'd been. A man his age, off on a romp with his secretary. Madness. It was over, by God, and he meant over. Then he found the letter Pearl had written Miriam pinned to his pillow. It looked as if Miriam had taken several stabs at it before securing it.

I know that Ignatius has spoken to you of me. The last thing I want is to come between a man and his wife. I know how traumatic talk of divorce can be and have stopped Ignatius every time he has talked of leaving you . . .

He had torn the thing into shreds and flushed it down the toilet. He had come home with a buzz on, but now he was clearheaded and sober. And frightened. He just wasn't the kind of man whose wife walked out on him. He was a Notre Dame man! He had to get Miriam back — but how could he unload Pearl?

It all became a great deal more complicated when a big guy in a towel confronted him in the club locker room after a phenomenally awful round.

"I remember you," the man said.

Iggie found his glasses and put them on, adopting his professional smile.

"From South Bend."

"A Domer!" Iggie stood, managing to catch his towel before he would look like Adam in Eden, before the fall. "What year?"

"I lived in Alumni Hall."

"So did I!"

"I know."

"So what's your name?"

"George Wintheiser."

Iggie nearly dropped his towel again. Pearl's name was Wintheiser.

"Weren't you on the team?" he managed to say.

Wintheiser bent and looked him in the steamy glasses. "Leave my wife alone."

He went off to his locker, and Iggie darted back into the shower. Could all great Neptune's ocean wash this guilt from off his soul? He stood under water as cold as he could stand. He warmed it up a little and remained under the shower. He was still wearing his glasses. Oh, to hell with it. He wanted to make damned sure Wintheiser had dressed and left before he got out of the shower.

"I met your husband," he said to Pearl the next day.

"I'm getting a divorce."

"Come on, you're Catholic."

"You sound like George."

"What happened between you two, Pearl?" He tried for a concerned tone, the tone of a man anxious to help her in her troubles.

"What did he say happened?"

"No need to go into that."

It was an inspiration. He had transferred his panic to Pearl.

"I think he wants to get back together with you."

"Did he say that?"

"Pearl, he spoke in confidence. One Notre Dame man to another."

"To hell with Notre Dame."

"You can't mean that."

This time her sobbing did not unnerve him. He patted her shoulder and managed to keep his hand from sliding down her back.

"Give it another chance, Pearl."

It worked! Well, at least it cooled any ardor Pearl had felt for him. She apparently thought he knew all sorts of things he didn't. Ignorance is power.

With half his problem settled, he began

telephoning Miriam regularly at her mother's.

"What did you tell her, sweetheart?"

"Is that all that bothers you?"

"Come home. Please."

He sent her flowers, using their regular florist. He asked her to come to the Boston College game with him.

That was before the disastrous season began. Iggie would never have admitted it to himself, but he welcomed the vast distraction of the string of defeats with which the Notre Dame season began. He felt betrayed rather than a traitor. It was a good warm feeling. He got the fellow who had computerized his billing system to set up the Web site CheerCheerForOldNotreDame. The response was terrific. He flew back and forth to South Bend, a man with a mission. Charlie Weis had become his scapegoat.

10

Rimini was surprised and flattered that Wintheiser even knew that he had once been on the team, a member of the sacrificial squad that the varsity team played against in preparation for games. Nonetheless, aching, covered with mud and grass stains, the young Rimini had hobbled from the practice field on those long-ago afternoons, his helmet swinging from his hand, with the sense that he was an integral part of Notre Dame football. One step up from a tackling dummy, but what the hell, it had prepared him for life. He had never been able to duplicate that sense of exhausted achievement.

"Where would we have been without you guys?" Wintheiser had said in response to Rimini's self-deprecating remark. It was a sports banquet kind of remark, but Rimini appreciated it nonetheless. He had reached an age when he grasped at any laurel offered.

Not that he and the enormous Wintheiser had been students at the same time. Wintheiser was fifteen, twenty years younger. Still, there seemed an easy camaraderie between them when Wintheiser came to Rimini's office in Decio.

"Not many former players on the faculty, are there?"

Rimini might have said something unforgivable, his loyalties pulled between memories of those long-ago afternoons when he had been buffeted and knocked about by larger men and the ethereal ivory tower of academe to which one was admitted on the basis of brain, not brawn.

"Not many Renaissance men," Rimini replied.

Wintheiser was looking at Rimini's framed degrees, prominently displayed on what little wall space the office had.

"My degree is from the University of Chicago," Wintheiser said.

"Didn't you graduate from here?"

"I meant my doctorate."

Doctorate? Chicago? "What was your field?"

"Ancient languages. Hittite, mainly."

"Hittite! What do you do with that?"

"Not much. I helped my director put together his Hittite dictionary."

"And then?"

"I'm a commentator on ESPN. I'm surprised you didn't know that."

Rimini felt as if he had flunked a test. ESPN! It was a channel Rimini loathed, all those chattering panels, old jocks breaking one another up, pontificating about coming games, at last above the fray where no umpire would throw a flag if they made mistakes. "Of course," he said weakly, and then wished he hadn't.

"My main income is from commercials."

"So you're back for the game," Rimini said, trying to regain his sense of ease with this giant of a man. Hittite, ESPN, commercials — what was the world coming to?

"What do you make of all the agitation about the team?" Wintheiser asked.

The team. Our team. Rimini had put his guest in his reading chair, legs crossed, huge shoes on display, and himself at his desk. The whistles of yesteryear, the crack and thump of padded body hitting padded body, seemed to echo in the office.

"Adversity is a tough school."

Wintheiser liked that. "Absolutely. Those kids are playing their hearts out, and what thanks do they get? Self-appointed experts.

Know-it-alls. It's like ESPN. You ever watch Kornheiser?"

It was a rhetorical question.

"So what are we going to do about it?" This was not a rhetorical question.

"I suspect you have some ideas."

Wintheiser had ideas. He knew about Lipschutz's demand that football be dropped. He knew about Iggie Willis's Web site.

"Don't forget the Weeping Willows."

"Who are they?"

"Concerned alumni." Rimini said it with a sneer. "They're shocked — shocked — at the new Notre Dame. First it was the *Vagina Monologues.*"

"What a bunch of garbage."

Wintheiser seemed to mean the play. Rimini let it go. "Then it was the percentage of Catholics on the faculty."

"Is that a problem?"

"They seem to think so."

"I can't believe what has happened to the Catholic Church," Wintheiser said through clinched teeth. "Libertine priests, annulments . . ." He seemed to have run out of breath.

"Now they want to know how many Catholics are on the football team. And how many Irish."

"You're kidding."

"I wish I were. How many Catholics were on the team when you played?"

"We always went to Mass together on Saturday mornings. In the chapel at Moreau Seminary."

Rimini had forgotten that practice, which had apparently gone the way of many others that had once characterized football at Notre Dame.

"Lou came. The whole coaching staff."

"I wonder if there are any Catholics on the team now?"

"There are no atheists in foxholes."

They observed a moment of silence.

"So what exactly are your ideas, George?" Or should he have said Dr. Wintheiser?

"The best defense is a good offense."

Rimini nodded. Even clichés have their role to play in polite conversation. He wondered if Wintheiser could translate his remark into Hittite.

What Wintheiser thought would be helpful was to make fun of the critics, lampoon them, hold them up to ridicule.

"You know any kids on these alternative campus papers?"

"As a matter of fact, I do."

"Good. Let's unleash them on these yo-yos. Cartoons, funny names, the whole thing. Picket their classes. Kids will know what to do."

"I'll get right on it."

Wintheiser rose. Standing, he need only lift his arms and he could touch the ceiling.

"Here's my cell phone number," Wintheiser said, putting a card on the desk. "Keep me posted."

Alone, without the thought that he and Wintheiser were acting as a team, he wondered how he could implement Wintheiser's idea. *Advocata Nostra* was out, and the other conservative paper. The *Observer*? Forget it. Then he had it. *Common Sense.* They were furious with the efforts of Weeping Willow to turn back the clock as far as Catholicism went. Did they give a damn about football? Then he remembered the several cutting remarks about Roger Knight that had appeared in *Common Sense* . . . and Roger's name had appeared on the list of professors supporting Lipschutz. How to approach them? Ah. Gordie Finlayson was the faculty advisor of *Common Sense.* His poems often appeared in its pages. Finlayson nursed a deep hatred for all chaired professors. Maybe that had been the reason for those slams at Knight.

He would talk to Finlayson. Let the campaign begin.

11

It should have been easier to track down football players to interview, but Bartholomew Hanlon found them an elusive bunch. Their size alone should have made them easy to spot, but then many of them allegedly went around campus in electric carts, so their height was hidden. Did they eat in dining halls with mere mortals?

"Why do you ask?" The young man's shaved head gave him an infantile look, as if he were still awaiting his first growth.

"I'm a reporter."

The bald one backed away. "We're not supposed to talk with reporters."

"You're on the team?"

Bartholomew's incredulous tone didn't help. "I'm the kicker."

"Of course. I didn't recognize you out of uniform."

Bartholomew had fallen into conversation with John Wesley just outside the South

Dining Hall. Now he led him to a bench, where Wesley reluctantly sat down. Bartholomew got out a notebook.

"Nothing about football."

"Absolutely not."

Bartholomew realized that he was being less than truthful. In fact, he was lying. He had got hold of a team roster and then checked out the names in the campus phone book. Few players seemed to live on campus. Wesley, however accidentally encountered, was thus a real prize.

"How did you become a kicker?"

Wesley started to rise. "I mean it. Coach doesn't want us giving interviews."

"I don't blame him."

"What do you mean?" Wesley sat again and looked at him narrowly. "No games. We can't talk about them."

"No football, period. What hall do you live in?"

That got the ball rolling. Wesley was from Nebraska, someplace west of Omaha that Bartholomew had never heard of. "Why did you come to Notre Dame?"

"They came to me." Wesley raised a hand as if to stop himself.

"What attracted you to a Catholic school?"

"What do you mean?"

101

"Well, after all, this is the premier Catholic university."

A look of pain spread over Wesley's face. "You sound like my mother."

"I have a cold." Wesley's eyes widened, and then he roared with laughter. Bartholomew had made a friend. "What about your mother?"

"She's worried I'll become a Catholic."

"You're not Catholic?"

"No! Methodist."

"I've heard of it."

"Heard of it! It's one of the largest denominations. We're all over the country. Do you know who started the most universities in this country? The Methodists, that's who."

"I suppose your mother wanted you to go to one of those."

"Oh, no. They're not Methodist anymore."

"How many Methodists on the team?"

"Only five."

"So few among so many Catholics! No wonder your mother worries."

"Ha."

Bartholomew waited, but that seemed to be it. "They don't pester you?"

"About religion? Football is our religion."

"I'll tell your mother."

Wesley's laughter was delayed but dependable.

"How many Catholics are on the team?"

"How should I know."

"Someone told me the team goes to Mass together before games."

"Come on."

"It's not true?"

"I never heard of it."

"How about the coaches?" He put out a hand to stop Wesley from rising. "I mean religionwise."

"Ask them."

"Take a guess."

Wesley's roommate, John Foster Natashi, from darkest Africa, was also on the team. He was majoring in computer science. He seemed to think that Bartholomew was one of the tutors provided athletes and had come to help John with his homework. When Bartholomew identified himself, Natashi admitted he had never heard of *Advocata Nostra.*

"It's one of those giveaways," Wesley explained.

"Do you buy the *Observer*?" Bartholomew had bristled at this description of his paper.

"I see your point."

"Actually, you do. It comes out of your fees."

Natashi had withdrawn to his side of the room and was now kneeling on a little rug. His head tipped over, touching the floor, and he remained motionless but not sound-less for several minutes.

"It doesn't take him long."

"Not a Methodist, I gather?"

Natashi was indeed done with his prayers in a few minutes and rolled up the little rug. Bartholomew asked him where he had gone to high school.

"Prep school. Choate."

"And you ended up at Notre Dame?"

"We have a devotion to Jesus' mother."

"At Choate?"

"I am a wide receiver."

"He'll be drafted before his senior year," Wesley said proudly.

"Maybe the war will be over by then."

"He's kidding," Wesley said.

"Many Muslims on the team?"

"Only one. So far."

"Ah."

"Islam is the religion of the future."

"Tell it to the Methodists."

Bartholomew left the roommates arguing amicably. Were two players a sufficient basis to write another article? They would have to do.

12

They met in Lipschutz's hideaway office in Brownson. Wessel, Francoeur, and Fitz-James, what Lipschutz thought of as his steering committee, were surprised and delighted to find that Lipschutz had secured the names of Otto Bird and Roger Knight for the petition that Notre Dame withdraw from college football, turn its back on the creeping professionalization of the game, and regain its soul. This was all bunk, of course. Lipschutz did hate football, but because he saw it as draining off huge sums of money that might have been more meaningfully spent elsewhere — for example, on the center he had proposed to the provost that, under the direction of Lipschutz, would put the university unquestionably among the leading research universities of the land. Ever since he had submitted the proposal the previous spring, complete with projected budgets for five years and suggestions as to where the building to house it could be erected, there had been foot-dragging from the main building.

There were those who might have thought that the campaign he was now leading against the Notre Dame football program would spell the ultimate quietus of his dreamed-of center. Lipschutz had thought through the matter carefully, listening to all his arguments and finding them good. What he would engineer was an inescapable either/or. Was the university serious about becoming a leading research university? If so, how did this comport with the madness of exploiting young men on the football field, young men who could scarcely be called students in any serious sense, and at who knew what cost of revenue?

"Horst," FitzJames said. "Football brings in millions."

"That is the story."

"You don't believe it?"

"A better question is, where does such money go? Into the professionalization of all the other sports in which the university engages."

"That is their story," Wessel agreed.

"So what is Notre Dame to be? A farm team of the professional football leagues or an honest-to-God university?"

107

The steering committee liked it. The next order of business concerned the means of publicizing their demand.

"The blimp that flies over the stadium during football games runs ads on its sides."

"Hardly appropriate."

"A vigil in front of the Main Building?"

"Or at the athletic department."

"The decision will not be theirs," Lipschutz decided. "Let us consider the Main Building."

It was one of Lipschutz's guilty secrets that he loved the movie *Patton.* He owned a copy, and he had watched it more times than he would want his friends, or enemies, to know. A scene from the movie sprang before his eyes. Patton in Palermo, in battle helmet and jodhpurs, silver pistols on his belt, boots gleaming, mounts a great stairway at the top of which the archbishop awaits him. A steely-eyed glance at the prelate and then, genuflecting, George Patton kisses the episcopal ring. The onlookers go wild with ecstacy. What a coup! Was it not possible that, analogously, after mustering at the foot of the stairway leading up to the entrance of the Main Building, the president and his minions, moved by the placards, would appear at the top of the stairs? Horst Lipschutz with a solemn expression mounts the stairs, gives the president a Patton look, and then presents him with the cogent and eloquent petition. No genuflecting or kissing of rings, of course. No need for that. What was the president if not *primus inter pares* — if indeed that?

Lipschutz liked it. It only remained to pick an appropriate day — and to go over and over the petition on which Lipschutz had been working since it first occurred to him that the present dismal football season represented a golden opportunity to strike while the administration, whose fingerprints were all over the appointment of this outrageously overpaid coach, was reeling and vulnerable.

13

After the Boston College game, Neil Genoux had accompanied the presidential
party to the fourteenth floor of the library
for what was to have been a celebration of a
reversal of the abysmal fortunes of the
football season. But Notre Dame had lost
yet again. Ignominiously. Genoux's reminder that Boston College had been beating Notre Dame regularly in recent years
was not well received. Notre Dame had lost
a game that, in the opinion of those gathered
in the aerie on top of the library, with its
magnificent views of less than magnificent
things to view, Notre Dame should have
won.

"He should have switched quarterbacks,"
opined W. T. Gravitas, a member of the
board.

The presidential response to this was a
shy grin and a dipping of the head. Genoux
wondered what the presidential response to

Armageddon would be.

"Is Roger Knight here?" Genoux was asked by Mimi O'Toole, the wiry wife of an obese husband who was on the board for purely monetary reasons.

"Do you know him?"

"Know him! I wish I did. You should bring us into contact with distinguished members of the faculty."

Genoux thought of the mopey poet and failed novelist who had been trundled out to the board as a fair sample of the faculty. Dear God!

"How long will you be here?"

"Francis is flying off at the crack of dawn."

"And you?"

"Arrange a meeting with Roger Knight and I will stay forever."

The woman began to dilate on Baron Corvo, a depraved and fascinating figure of whom she was dying to learn.

"Done," said Neil Genoux. "You're in the Morris Inn? I will notify you of arrangements." Baron Corvo seemed an infinitely more attractive topic than whether or not another quarterback could have reversed the team's dismal showing and filled the hearts of students, alumni, and some faculty with the sweet taste of victory. "Tell me about Corvo."

"I know next to nothing about him. That's why I want to meet Professor Knight."

Genoux found the subject soporific but preferable to talking about who should be quarterback. He assured Mimi that he would arrange a meeting with Professor Roger Knight, and then, the moment seeming propitious, he escaped.

Descending in the elevator and emerging into the great out-of-doors, Genoux stopped and filled his lungs with the tonic air of autumn. The dim now-odious hulk of the stadium was visible to the south, but he ignored it. It had had its moment and failed. He went around the pond, where in spring ducklings floated, and found a bench, on which he collapsed. The great mural at the front of the library was illumined, Christ, the teacher. The suggestion seemed to be that Jesus was a professor manqué. Dear God.

Into each soul must creep temptations to think that everything that has guided one's life hitherto, unquestioned certitudes, is a packet of lies. So it was that, to Neil Genoux, all the unexamined axioms that guided his days seemed suddenly in the dock. He did not know whether to weep or cry. What is he to Hecuba or Hecuba to him? A host of dubiously relevant quotes

112

drifted across his mind.

And who in hell was Baron Corvo?

The bench on which he sat faced east. Somewhere in the gloaming was graduate student housing and the apartment where Roger Knight dwelt with his brother. Genoux knew these things as a bombardier knows the terrain of his target. He rose, steadied himself, and plunged eastward, Knightward, Rogerward. A discerning ear might have descried an off-key rendition of the fight song issuing from his smiling lips.

The gathering at the Knight apartment could not have been more happenstance, or, perhaps in a better interpretation, providential. Genoux's knock had not been acknowledged, but as he stood waiting the door burst open and a figure reeled into the night, took up his stance on the lawn, and, addressing the night sky, bellowed, *"Quousque tandem abutere, Catalina, patientia nostra?"* After throwing up, he returned through the door from which he had exited. Genoux followed him in. Clearly this was not a time when the niceties of visitation were observed.

The scene he came upon might have been the incarnation of all his nightmares. Genoux was a willing agent of the administration. Whatever his wavering private views, he had endeavored to be a conscientious representative of those who had plucked him from the supposed obscurity of nineteenth-century literature and put him down at the alleged pinnacle of power. Like the good steward of the gospel, he had learned to lie and cheat for his masters. Now, here, in the Knight apartment, he found himself surrounded by the enemies of the administration. Never had anonymity felt so desirable, and indeed he seemed to have twisted the ring of Gyges on his finger and become invisible to the enemies of the administration for whom he toiled.

In one corner of the room, a man sipping a soft drink was listening to an enormous man who had to be Roger Knight. Genoux knew him by reputation; he had been pointed out to him from a third-floor window of the Main Building, guiding his golf cart among the students on the walk. Within a few years, the man had become a legend. He seemed to know more about the place to which he had come than those who had spent a lifetime there. How could such alleged genius be housed in that massive body? He had caught Roger's eye and was beckoned forward.

"Father Genoux, isn't it?"

Genoux was amazed. They had never met. He had no reason to think that Roger even knew he existed. "*The Ethics of Austen.*" The huge man made a little face and wagged a finger.

"You've read it?" This was Genoux's doctoral dissertation, rotting as he would have thought like Miss Havisham's wedding cake in some obscure corner of the library.

"I found it interesting. For a dissertation, that is."

The other man said, "I am Francis Parkman. Are you the Genoux who works in the president's office?"

Startled, Genoux laughed a nervous laugh. "Work in the president's office? That's an oxymoron."

Roger Knight, at least, appreciated this.

"You have a bad habit of not answering letters."

What would he say if he knew the letters were filed under CRANKS? Parkman, chairman of the Weeping Willow Society, did not look at all like Genoux had imagined.

"Not the ethics of Austen," Roger chided.

"I wish I could discuss it now," Genoux lied, "but the fact is I dropped by to ask Professor Knight if he could possibly meet the wife of one of the trustees on Monday."

"Then you do accommodate some

115

wishes."

"Mimi O'Toole. She's staying in the Morris Inn. She wants to talk about Baron Corvo."

"For lunch?" Roger asked.

"That would be perfect."

"Only if we can be served on the patio."

"I'll let her know."

Mission accomplished, he wanted to flee, but Parkman was now positioned in a way that would make that difficult.

"Father, know this. We are quite serious, and we intend to get the information we ask for. We intend to get responses to the sensible suggestions we have made. We are not in the grip of some momentary pique. For many of us, if this is the last thing we do in our lives, we will be content. So please don't think that our society will fade away like a football season."

"I promise to pass this on," Genoux said.

"Threats are never seemly, particularly threats of litigation. I speak as a judge. But you might consider that there are many strange new laws and even stranger judicial decisions. Surely you wouldn't want to be sued by alumni whose desires are the good of this institution?"

All this was said in the calmest of tones, Parkman's voice raised only because of the level of noise in the apartment. In self-defense, Genoux took his hand and shook it vigorously. He nodded at Roger.

"Monday."

"Did you say Mimi O'Toole, Father?" Parkman asked.

"Yes."

Genoux waited, but there was nothing further.

14

Only after persistent questioning had Father Carmody told Iggie the line from the Cataline Orations.

"Did you pass that class?"

"Father, I loved Latin."

"Not a reciprocated passion. You better go easy with that stuff." The priest nodded at Iggie's glass. There was some giant who kept filling it up. Iggie's glasses were in his shirt pocket, and even apart from the alcohol he had consumed, the world would have been blurred.

"At this time of night it goes down like water."

"That's what it largely is. It's the rest that does you in."

"Not Iggie Willis."

"Doesn't your profession require a steady hand?"

The image of Pearl drifted by Iggie's clouded mind, followed by Miriam, wearing a disapproving look not unlike Father Carmody's. Iggie fought the impulse to pour out his troubles to the priest. This wasn't the place or the time. He must do that, however, before he headed home.

"It starts with *quo,*" he prompted.

Father Carmody recited the line then. Murmuring it over and over, not wanting to lose it, Iggie headed for the door. Outside, on the lawn, addressing some constellation he couldn't have named, he shouted the Ciceronian line to the stars. The night air had the odd effect of making him feel drunk. He was drunk. Whoops, here it comes. He bent over and retched helplessly, managing to miss his trousers but not his shoes.

When he was sure it was over, he plunged back inside, looking for the bathroom.

"You left your glass."

The giant again. Iggie took the glass, full to the brim. A hair of the dog. This was more like a pelt. A belt. He was laughing as he headed for the bathroom.

A very bedraggled dentist looked out at him from the mirror. Are you really drunk if you know you are? Thank God he had been outside when he threw up. He blamed it all on the loss that afternoon. He liked a drink, sure, but getting drunk was not in his repertoire. It was being back on campus that explained it, that and the loss to Boston College. It had taken Iggie years to like Doug Flutie, the first BC quarterback to have humiliated Notre Dame.

Iggie slipped out of his loafers and rinsed them off in the sink. Good as new. He had trouble slipping into them again, but he managed. Don't underestimate good old Iggie Willis. He picked up his drink and left the bathroom. The giant seemed to be waiting for him.

"Wintheiser," he replied when Iggie asked him who he was.

Wintheiser! Pearl's husband. As Iggie thought of returning to the bathroom and locking the door, he put on his glasses. This guy was two heads taller and had the body of a linebacker, but then that is what he had been. Wintheiser was nodding.

"I didn't recognize you in clothes."

Nothing. Just a steely stare.

"The locker room? The club? When you threatened me?"

"Did I threaten you?"

How in the hell could he put this? *Take your wife, I'm through with her?* "Look," he began.

Wintheiser put up a hand, a huge hand; he could have gripped Iggie's head in it like a football.

"You're right," Iggie said with relief. "Let bygones be bygones. What did you think of the game?"

"I think they ought to fire the fans." No change of expression, no twinkle in the eye. He looked at Iggie as if there were something on his face. He dabbed with his handkerchief. There had been something on his face.

"I threw up," he explained to Wintheiser.

"Now you have your second wind."

That turned out to be true. He took a long pull on his drink and found it bracing.

"I've got to sit down."

"You drive here?"

"On a game day? You're kidding."

"Where you staying?"

"The Morris Inn."

"I'll take you there."

"Leahy's would be better than this."

"You got everything?"

"You know, George, I'm glad we got together like this. I've wanted to call. The trouble is, what could I say?"

Outside there was an electric cart, and Wintheiser helped him get into the passenger seat.

"Where did you get this?"

"The athletic department."

Soundlessly the cart began to move. Iggie

121

put back his head and looked at the night sky. This time he didn't shout the line. *Quousque tandem abutere, Catalina, patientia nostra?*

"What's it mean?"

"How long will you abuse our patience, Catalina."

"Who's Catalina?"

"An island off the California coast."

Was the guy dumb or something? Still, it was nice of him to offer this ride back to the Morris Inn.

"I'm thinking of serenading Charlie Weis with that line."

15

After the game Masses are said in various chapels around the campus, as well as in Sacred Heart Basilica and the Stepan Center, a convenience for travelers, since this vigil Mass fulfilled their Sunday obligation. There were many, too many, expressions of the thought that a requiem Mass would be appropriate after such a loss. Before these worshippers set out for home, the bulk of the visiting fans would have been efficiently directed on their way by campus and local police. With nightfall, revelers subsided and something like peace covered the campus lawns, the trees, the residence buildings. Already, in the stadium, the work of cleaning up had begun, and with morning other crews would remove the debris that littered the campus.

Notre Dame is the largest local employer, and provides as well a number of temporary tasks associated with football. There were the ushers in the stadium, those who guided visitors in the parking lots, police from around and about who helped keep things orderly, vendors of various sorts, and the campus cleanup crew.

It was not a cold day, but Bridget Sokolowski wore an extralarge windbreaker and a cap with an oversized bill. Nothing odd there; it was the huge sunglasses that surprised, but then Bridget both needed the money this temporary employment afforded and was ashamed to be engaged in such menial labor. A temporary member of the underclass. No one she cared about knew that this was how she spent Sunday mornings after a Notre Dame home game, cleaning up the darned campus. It was something any nitwit could do. There was no skill involved at all. It was just the mechanical act of picking up and cramming into plastic bags paper, Styrofoam, cups, plates, bottles, whatever. She felt like a bag lady.

The crew she was with moved down the mall westward toward Rockne Memorial. When they got there, they took a break. Bridget moved away from the others and sat on a little wall, looking toward the golf course. Just below her was the practice putting green. The man lying on it seemed to have assumed the posture of the little leprechaun, the Notre Dame mascot. For a moment, she wondered if it was the mascot, but the man wasn't wearing that elfin outfit. Imagine sleeping outside like that. He had probably passed out and didn't know where he was.

"Whatcha looking at?"

It was the girl they called Chita. Bridget shrugged, but she turned away and felt that her eyes would draw Chita's to the drunk asleep on the practice green.

"Look at the guy on the grass," Chita cried.

"Passed out."

"I wonder. Let's go see what's going on."

"Not me."

"Hey, you found him."

"What do you mean, found him?"

"Well, I'm going to take a look."

A minute later Chita's shriek lifted from the putting green and the whole crew rushed to see what was the matter. But not Bridget. She left her plastic bag full of trash and hurried across the mall, anxious to get the hell out of there. The body on the putting green spelled trouble, and Bridget was not eager to get involved in any publicity that would reveal to her friends how she spent the Sunday after home games.

125

■ ■ ■ ■

PART TWO

■ ■ ■ ■

1

The chief of the cleaning crew alerted campus security, and when the patrol car arrived, most of the crew lost interest and drifted away. This break was turning into a long one, and they intended to enjoy it. There were some among them whose relations with the police had not always been happy. The rest just wanted to avoid whatever trouble the dead man on the putting green represented. Except Chita.

"I found him," she told one of the cops.

"Yeah?"

"We were standing up there, sitting on that wall, and we looked down and there he was."

"We?"

"Bridget noticed him first."

"Where's Bridget?"

Bridget could not be found. The cop let his partner, a real fatty, look after the body. He wanted Chita to sit in the patrol car and tell him all about it. He wanted to get in back with her, but she put the kibosh on that.

"You up front, me back here."

"Maybe you should contact your lawyer."

"Lawyer? What are you talking about?"

"Anything you say may be held against you." He made it sound dirty.

"You've been watching too much TV."

"So what did you hit him with?"

Chita opened the back door, but the cop stopped her. "Hey, I'm just kidding around."

"Do corpses affect you that way?"

"Only dead ones." But he stopped his eyebrows from dancing before they really got started. He was kind of cute.

"Tell me all about it."

"In my own words?"

"Just so it's English."

"No habla español?"

"Let me see your green card."

"I was born in Indiana!"

"No kidding."

"I went to St. Joe High School."

His face lit up. "What year?"

"Don't tell me they let you in."

"It was getting out that was the problem."

"How long you been a cop?"

"A few years."

"What do you do for a living?"

"Listen to killers trying to deflect me from my interrogation."

Finally he got serious, and she told him what she had seen and done.

"You came right down to inspect the body?"

"I wanted to see what was wrong with him."

"What was wrong?"

"He was dead."

"How did you figure that out? Did you try giving him first aid? You know, mouth to mouth."

He was back to being a stand-up comic. His name was on the label sewn above the right pocket of his shirt. Larry Douglas.

"What's your wife's name, Larry?"

"Mrs. Douglas."

"That figures. That her guarding the body?"

"I'm not married!"

"That figures, too."

He was kind of nice when he wasn't playing cop.

"What year were you in at St. Joe?" he asked.

"1066."

"What's a good-looking smartie like you doing on a cleanup crew?"

"Meeting dumb cops."

"Let's go find Bridget."

First he had to call in. Chita listened. How ordinary it sounded. Dead white male, drunk, fortyish, must have been at the game Saturday. He had to repeat what he said about the Notre Dame towel.

"That's right. Stuffed in his mouth."

Larry was asked who the dead man was.

"Ignatius Willis."

Campus security called Father Genoux, and he immediately put in a call to Father Carmody at Holy Cross House. Despite the hour, the old priest sounded bright and chipper. Probably he still said his Mass at the crack of dawn.

"They found the body of Ignatius Willis on the putting green next to Rockne."

"Dead?"

"Yes."

"He was at the Knights' party after the game."

"I know."

"Who reported it?"

"I just got a call from campus security."

"Come and get me."

Genoux was halfway to Holy Cross House before he realized that he hadn't hesitated a minute to obey the old priest. Well, this was something he hoped to dump in Carmody's

132

lap. If there was any way to prevent this from blowing up into unwelcome publicity, Carmody would know.

He was standing under the overhang when Genoux arrived, and he skipped out to the car and got in.

"Where's the body?"

"Where they found it."

"Let's get going."

At the putting green, Father Carmody went immediately to the body and knelt beside it, head bowed. He was praying. He lifted his hand in blessing and then let it lie on the dead man's shoulder. He used the shoulder to get himself upright again. He looked around, and it was clear he was relieved to find that the cop on the job was a young fellow named Larry Douglas. "You check the hole?"

"For what?"

"A ball. This is a putting green."

Apparently a joke. Carmody listened while Douglas told him what he knew.

"Who else knows?"

"The cleaning crew found him."

Carmody frowned. "And you called it in?"

"I told Bernice to let Father Genoux know."

"She talk to anyone else?"

"Bernice?"

"I don't know her. Let's keep a lid on this, Larry. For now."

"What about the body?"

For an awful moment, Genoux thought Carmody would suggest getting rid of it — bury it, drop it in the lake.

"No more harm can come to him lying there." He turned to Genoux. "You got a cell phone, Father?"

Taking it, he punched a number with slow deliberation and then seemed to wonder which end to put to his ear. He listened, frowning out at the golf course, or what was left of it. The back nine had been built on; only the front remained. Genoux knew that Carmody did not like the new course north of campus that had cost a bundle to develop.

"Roger? Father Carmody. Is Phil there?"

2

"You want to come along, Roger?" Phil asked when he told his brother why Father Carmody had called.

"I have to go to Mass."

Of course. Only Roger was Catholic, converted during his time at Princeton. He had enigmatically likened this to F. Marion Crawford's conversion while he was in India, after having been brought up in Rome in the shadow of the Vatican. Phil had learned not to ask Roger to explain such remarks. Phil believed in God, of course — someone had to be in charge of all this — but the niceties of religious belief had never drawn him.

"They will," Roger said. Nothing smug about it, just a statement.

"Willis was among our guests last night, Phil."

"I know."

Phil did not want to think about that

135

party; he did not want to remember how much he had drunk. The party had roared on for hours after Father Carmody left, and it continued to roar on in Phil's aching head.

"Call me after church," Phil said, putting on a jacket.

There was no point in calling Roger. Even when he had his cell phone with him, he never turned it on until he wanted to use it.

When he went through the campus gate, saluting the guard, Phil wondered if she knew a dead body had been found on campus. He doubted it. Father Carmody had indicated that he didn't want anyone spreading the alarm, at least not yet.

Larry Douglas and his partner, Laura, were crouched at the edge of the putting green nearest the road. The two priests were standing by the body. Laura had put a piece of clear plastic on the ground.

"What are you doing?"

"Laura has found some footprints." Larry crossed his eyes. No wonder. There were footprints all over the putting surface. Maybe Laura should get a big piece of plastic and cover the whole thing.

"You mean that?" Larry asked.

For answer, Phil crossed his eyes.

Father Carmody unnecessarily pointed to the body on the grass.

"Any sign of violence, Father?"

"You're the detective. I assume you'll represent the university in this?"

Phil knelt and looked at the lifeless body of Iggie Willis. There were no marks on the face or chest. He carefully turned the body. Nothing there. So what had killed him?

"I took this from his mouth," Laura said, flourishing a little green towel with ND on it. It also had a metal-rimmed hole in one corner.

"From his mouth?"

"It was jammed in."

Was that how Iggie Willis had died? Phil held open one of the plastic bags he had brought, and Laura dropped it in.

"You think that's a murder weapon?" she asked.

"I don't know. He doesn't look as if he had died from asphyxiation, but I'm no doctor. We'd better call Jimmy Stewart."

Jimmy Stewart was a South Bend detective with whom Phil had worked previously, when some campus disturbance necessitated it and Father Carmody had enlisted Phil's now dormant private investigation agency. He was as much interested in the discretion he could count on as in Phil's professional expertise. Campus security had many members who had served on various police forces in the region, but they weren't equipped to conduct a murder investigation. If this was a murder.

"Last night he seemed to be trying to drink himself to death," Father Carmody said.

"I wonder how he got here from our apartment."

"He was staying in the Morris Inn."

"So why is he here?"

"Maybe he didn't know where he was."

And lay down here and stuffed a towel in his mouth? Phil dialed Jimmy's home number and waited out the enormous number of rings before the phone was answered.

"Jimmy? Philip Knight."

"Call me back later."

The phone went dead. Phil punched redial and wondered if he had interrupted something. Jimmy's wife had left him, out finding herself somewhere, but who knows what trouble a lonely single man can get into?

"Tell her I'm sorry," Phil said, when at last Jimmy answered again.

"Tell who?"

"Then you're alone?"

A pause. "Flattery will get you nowhere."

"Jimmy, we've got a body on the putting green next to Rockne Memorial. Any chance of your dropping by?"

"You got coffee there?"

"I will have. How about some dough-nuts?"

"And some juice. Tomato."

"Yes, sir."

Larry asked Laura to go fetch a breakfast for Jimmy and coffee for everyone else.

"I haven't eaten either," Phil said.

"You hear that, Laura?"

"Yes, master." She waddled away to the patrol car, taking off with a spin of wheels.

"I hope she doesn't obscure any foot-prints," Larry said. The two priests just looked at him. Who cared? Philip Knight understood him.

Father Carmody had taken the plastic bag into which Laura had put the green towel. "There's no reason to make a big thing of this, is there, Phil?"

Father Carmody's concern for the good name of Notre Dame was phenomenal. It pained him personally to hear criticism of the university in which he had spent his lifetime, unless of course he was doing the criticizing. Phil knew that the old priest would give much if Iggie Willis's death could be judged natural. Cardiac arrests on game days were not a rarity. Unfortunately, the green towel cast doubt on this possibility. Even if it hadn't been the cause of Willis's death, there was the puzzle of what the towel was doing jammed into his mouth.

Father Genoux took the occasion of the lull to leave, mumbling about concelebrating in Sacred Heart. Laura got back with the food before Jimmy came. He got out of his car, looking ruffled and unshaven. He started toward them and stopped before coming onto the putting green, staring silently down at the piece of plastic Laura had laid down. Then he came to look at the body.

"Know who he was?"

"His name is Ignatius Willis," Father Carmody said.

"He was at our party last night," Phil added.

"Well, he's dead, all right. I'll call in and have them come take the body away."

"They'll be able to tell if he died naturally, I trust," Father Carmody said.

Jimmy said, "Of course."

Phil took the plastic sack from the old priest and showed it to Jimmy.

"What about it?"

"It was found in his mouth."

"In his mouth."

Laura spoke up. "Just stuffed in. I took it out. It seemed the right thing to do."

Jimmy said nothing. He held the plastic sack to get a better looked at its contents.

"You know what it is, don't you?" he asked Phil.

"The kind of towel that hangs from a golf ball washer."

"Where's the nearest one?"

Father Carmody came with them. At Jimmy's request, so did Laura.

Larry Douglas, left to guard the body, was devastated. It was his dream to move from campus security to the South Bend police force, and he thought Jimmy Stewart favored this plan.

The ball washer was just off the first tee. A ball washer but no towel.

Jimmy put out his arms as they approached. "If this is where it came from, we don't want to muck up any prints."

Prints there were, many old ones, others seemingly fresh.

Jimmy told Laura to cover the area with plastic. "Let's hope one of these matches the ones you covered on the green."

Laura was aglow with the understated praise.

Father Carmody said, as they returned to the putting green, "Maybe we'll find Iggie Willis's shoe prints by that washer."

3

COACH CRITIC KILLED was the headline in the local paper, story by P. G. Grafton. He had written beneath that "Putting Out," but it had been deleted by Copey, his editor.

"Why?"

"It depends on how you pronounce it."

Copey explained the ambiguity, but Grafton, who seemed to have hidden behind a bush in Eden when the apple was eaten, did not understand. The explanation became more detailed. In the end, the editor settled for the suggestion "Putt-ing Out," and that is how it was printed.

Grafton was a self-made reporter, whose models would not have figured in any ordinary course of journalism. Not for him the weary train of w's — who, where, what, when, and the rest. Grafton did not write, he composed; he saw the facts that he was narrating through the medium of his imagination. Why else were they called the media?

The body on the putt-ing green on campus had been only a tragic object until Grafton googled the name Ignatius Stephen Willis and came upon the Web site CheerCheer-For*Old*NotreDame.com. He would not have described the inspiration that then came to him with the banality of a light bulb going on over his narrow, sparsely thatched head. Such an intuition was too sacred for that. Reading the Web site's passionate comments on the current Notre Dame football season and thinking of that body on the greensward — he looked up the word — something more compelling than logic linked the two beyond any doubt in the reportorial mind. A critic of Charlie Weis, a man who had rallied his fellow alumni into a virtual army of protest, demanding that the coach be sacked, had been definitively silenced.

The suggestion was made impressionistically, of course. Let the reader's engaged mind slide from one event as cause to the other as effect. Grafton thought of his method as Socratic. The reader could connect the dots. (In his mind, he deleted that cliché.) Only later did he learn that the prudent Copey had run the story by the paper's lawyer before giving his final okay. Such caution amused Grafton. If Notre Dame had been stung by the story, they certainly would not have drawn even more attention to it by protesting or threatening to go to law.

Grafton was particularly lucky that Feeney, the coroner, had reached a tentative verdict before his story achieved its final form. Until then, there had been ambiguity. The towel from the golf ball washer on the first tee of the old Burke course seemed an unlikely murder weapon, although Grafton was ready with a headline: THROWING IN THE TOWEL. There were no signs of violence on the body, Feeney explained to Grafton, reviewing his gruesome probing.

Feeney was a nervous little fellow who had been talked into running for the elective office of coroner in order to ensure that his father would continue to be favored by the local political bosses.

"I did a residency in pathology at Mayo's," Feeney said mournfully. "They wanted me back there on the staff."

"You could have been somebody?"

"How many pathologists do you know? It's not fame, Grafton. Not money either. I could have been rich in ten years in private practice. No, it was the admiration and approval of men I admired and wished to model myself after. It all went up in smoke."

144

"Is your father still working?"

"Well, he's drawing a salary."

"What do you make of that green towel?"

"How do you mean?"

"Why was it stuffed in his mouth?"

"Search me. All I know is it didn't kill him."

A light had begun to shine in Feeney's eyes, and Grafton knew they were coming to the big conclusion.

"Something toxic, Grafton. Something taken internally."

"Poison?"

"Do you drink?"

"Alcohol? Very, very rarely. It is the bane of my profession."

"Just about anything can kill, you know. Things usually taken in moderation, or in less than murderous doses. Think of drowning. Willis's body had as much alcohol as blood in it. You could call it a kind of suicide."

Feeney might want to call it that, only it turned out he wouldn't — what basis did he have? — but Grafton wanted murder. Somehow it all seemed to hinge on the green towel with ND on it that had been taken from the ball washer on the first tee.

Grafton had omitted from his story what he had wrung out of Stewart about the shoe prints. All it came down to was that prints by the ball washer matched the ones on the putting green that had fascinated Laura.

"That doesn't tell us whose shoes they are."

"Not Willis's?"

"None of his prints are among those around the ball washer."

"All you have to do is find a shoe that matches those prints."

"What a brilliant idea."

For a moment, Grafton had thought Stewart was serious.

4

On Monday, Roger went in his golf cart to
the Morris Inn, approaching it from the
rear. A huge tent erected to accommodate
the overflow of celebrating fans made it
impossible to see if Mimi O'Toole was waiting for him on the patio. He should have
called to confirm the luncheon date to
which he had agreed during the distractions
of their party Saturday night. Roger managed to maneuver his vehicle into the great
tent. He left it there and lumbered through
the tent. When he emerged onto the side-
walk leading to the patio, there were expressions of astonishment and at least one of
welcome on the face of a pretty little lady at
one of the tables. She raised her hand and
several pounds of jewelry slipped from her
wrist toward her elbow.

"Mrs. O'Toole?" She looked up at Roger
hovering over her, some alarm mixed with
the pleasure she took from the effect this

was having on the others there on the patio.

"Professor Knight!" she cried, like the starter at a tournament announcing the next player.

Roger with great concentration managed to get his nether half into the wrought-iron chair. A tight fit, a very tight fit. Not a chair for the endowed. Mimi O'Toole half rose to her feet, as if she meant to help him, but when he settled in she sat back down. Would he like a Bloody Mary? It was what she was having. From her glass, celery sprouted; pickles and olives floated about; two straws rose from the foliage.

"Is it nonalcoholic?" he asked. It might have been some vegetarian drink.

"It better not be. Such a weekend."

A harried waitress came to ask Roger what he would drink. The suggestion was iced tea. It seemed the path of least resistance. They ordered food then, too. "Diners on the patio are easily forgotten," Mimi explained. "Another of these," she said to the waitress, tapping her glass.

The further harried waitress scuttled away.

"Now then." Mimi crossed her arms on the table and leaned toward Roger. "I want to hear all about your book on Baron Corvo."

"I'm surprised you've even heard of it."

"If it hadn't been mentioned in your bio in the booklet identifying all the endowed professors, I never would have known of it."

Roger had no experience of the enthusiastic reader; his was scarcely the kind of book that called for personal appearances and signings.

"Did you know him personally, Professor?"

Roger was taken aback. Baron Corvo's misspent life had long been over before Roger's began.

"He lived in Venice, you know."

Mimi made a face and sat back. "I hate Venice." She leaned forward again and whispered, "The smell."

"There's some truth in that."

"Did he have children?"

It was clear that Mimi O'Toole knew nothing of Baron Corvo. If she had read his book, it must have been upside down. Desperate for an alternative topic, he asked her if she had known Iggie Willis. Her mouth dropped open and her pretty green eyes widened.

"Of course I knew him. He has been pestering us to join him in an effort to fire the coach. Such an excitable man. And he was a dentist."

"They're having difficulty locating the widow."

"Was it his heart?"

The coroner's verdict was not yet firm, but Roger thought the heart must have been involved in Iggie's death — by stopping, at least.

"Francis, my husband, has had a quadruple bypass. He's supposed to exercise and eat sensibly, but he just won't. He keeps saying, 'I could already be dead. Fifty years ago I would have been dead.' He says his life is like continuing the play after a flag has been thrown on the other team."

"That's good," Roger said.

"He says we should now call him OT."

"What does your husband do?"

She sat back. "Well, I'm not often asked that question." Then, after a moment, "Isn't it strange? The trustees don't know the faculty and the faculty don't know the trustees."

"You shouldn't judge the faculty by me."

Roger sat on for half an hour, feeling he was performing a favor for Father Genoux, doing his bit for Notre Dame, but it was a painful lunch. Mimi O'Toole was a lovely person in many ways, Roger was sure of that. There was an expensive look about her. Roger had no idea how old she was or what went on beneath her perhaps artfully blond hair. The green eyes were her best feature.

Two men emerged from the tent and came along the path to the patio.

"Frank!" Mimi cried as they approached. "Frank Parkman!"

Parkman introduced the man with him. Professor Rimini. Mimi then presented Roger to them.

"Oh, Mr. Parkman and I are old friends," Roger said.

"So are we," Mimi said.

At the moment, Roger was more interested in Rimini. Bartholomew Hanlon's interview had appeared in *Advocata Nostra.*

Rimini said they were getting together with other former players. It was time someone spoke up in defense of the team.

Parkman took the hand Mimi offered and held it perhaps a trifle longer than necessary. And then he and Rimini were gone.

"Why don't we have more alumni like that?" Mimi O'Toole sighed.

"You were students here together."

She hesitated. "Yes. We were here together."

5

"This makes us almost accomplices, Phil," Roger said when he had read the newspaper account of Willis's death.

"In suicide?"

"That isn't what it says."

"Grafton, Roger. Jimmy is staying with suicide. The guy drank himself to death. He was pouring it down as if there were no tomorrow. Well, for him, there wasn't."

"What about the towel?"

Phil didn't know. Jimmy Stewart didn't know. Feeney, the coroner, didn't know.

"He didn't choke to death," Feeney had said. From him that was a strong statement. His job put few demands on his medical knowledge, and he had become fascinated with the many logically possible explanations of events.

"Could he have stuffed it in his own mouth?"

Feeney's caution had returned. "He had

thrown up sometime before he died. His shoes."

"Just wiping his mouth," Jimmy suggested.

Jimmy didn't like it, and neither did Phil. Sometimes he wished he had followed Father Carmody's suggestion and gotten rid of the towel.

Roger became fascinated with the enigma of the towel from the ball washer on the first tee.

"Someone went up there to get it and brought it back to the putting green."

"Where Willis was probably already dead."

"That's guessing."

"The towel didn't kill him, Roger."

Somehow that towel seemed connected, not only with Willis's Web site, but with all the other agitation that had been going on because of the football team's losing streak.

It could not be said that Roger had slipped away from the party Saturday night, but he had gone off to bed without fanfare, put in earplugs, and was soon asleep. Thus he had no idea when Iggie Willis had left, or whether he had gone alone or not. Reading Grafton's story was thus somewhat like reading of events in the next county. With the great difference that Roger knew quite well that Iggie, who had arrived at the party less than sober, throughout the night had poured drink after drink into himself. Roger remembered that Father Carmody had chided him about it. Thank God, Iggie hadn't been driving. Even so, it was hard to imagine anyone in his condition covering the distance from the apartment to the practice putting green next to Rockne.

"How was your lunch, Roger?" Phil asked him Monday evening.

"Memorable."

6

"Like he was lining up a putt," Bingham said, tipping his head so it was parallel to the table.

"In the dark?"

"I always close my eyes when I putt," Horvath said.

"You haven't putted in years."

"The remark has cloacal connotations," Armitage Shanks said.

"Putt, putt," said Bingham.

"What?" Potts asked. He was deaf and refused to do anything about it except cup his ear.

"I had an uncle who died on the golf course," Horvath mused.

"He was drunk as a lord," Potts said out of his private world.

"My uncle?"

This lugubrious conversation at the Old Bastards table at the University Club had been triggered by Grafton's creative article in the local paper.

"I don't even believe the obituaries in that rag."

"You'd think the man had been killed."

"He doesn't quite say that."

"He doesn't quite say anything."

These ancient gentlemen, now emeriti, had graced the faculty in what they all agreed was a better time, all but Bingham, who had taught law and had a contrary streak. They were either single or had lost their wives ("Or both," Bingham amended) and had lived into a time they did not understand. When most of them had arrived, there were three or four thousand students and fewer than half the buildings, and those now the least gaudy on campus. Current members of their respective departments did not know them; they were strangers in a strange land, a group of incompatible old men who took mordant comfort in one another's company. The club and their twice-weekly luncheons there had become a refuge and a tradition. Now the club, the one place on campus where they were still known and more or less welcomed, was scheduled to be razed.

Debbie came to the table. "Okay, which one of you did it?"

"Rephrase the question," Bingham suggested.

Debbie sat. She supposed there was some psychological explanation of it, but she liked these old guys. "The corpse on the putting green." She laughed. "That sounds like Agatha Christie."

"He was drunk as a lord," Potts said again.

"At the Algonquin table they're talking about his Web site."

Half a dozen pairs of eyes looked at her, waiting.

"On the Web. The computer. The World Wide Web."

"Ah, what a tangled web we weave . . ." Shanks intoned.

"It's a way of getting in touch with the alumni," Debbie said. "He was demanding that Weis be fired."

"Who's Weis?"

"So soon old and so late Weis."

"What do our distinguished colleagues at the Algonquin table say about this Web site?"

"They think it's a nutty effort, but they like it."

"Fire them all," Potts said. "Tear down all the buildings. Tear down the damned stadium while they're at it."

"You're thinking of Lipschutz," Debbie said.

"I hope not."

"He wants the athletic programs abandoned. Back to amateur sports."

"Who's Lipschutz?" Horvath asked.

"One of the young men."

Debbie gave up. Lipschutz was as old as her father.

"Maybe you should sign on with the Weeping Willows."

"There is a willow grows aslant a brook . . ." Shanks again.

"How about another round?" Debbie suggested as she rose.

"On the house?"

"Oh, you can have them right here."

Rhythmically she walked away, her graceful movements registered by six pairs of weak eyes that, for a moment, were filled with memories of better times indeed.

It was over that unlooked-for extra round of drinks that Armitage Shanks made his suggestion.

"Everyone is protesting and demonstrating," he first observed.

"Madness," Bingham said.

"No doubt. But there can be method in madness. Who has a greater grievance than we?"

His table companions nodded in agreement, although whether they were in agreement as to what their greater grievance might be was unclear.

"This club," Shanks went on. An ice cube had got into his mouth when he took a pull on his drink, and he spat it back into the glass. "Are we to sit complacently by until they arrive with the wrecking ball? Are we to go as lambs to the slaughter. *Allons, enfants!*"

"What?" Potts asked.

"We can chain someone to the front door."

"Who?"

"Potts?"

"Gentlemen," Armitage Shanks said with some solemnity. "This is a time for solidarity. We must act as one."

"Doing what?"

"Let's ask Debbie."

7

Frank Parkman was in far-off California when the new issue of *Advocata Nostra* arrived, but what are several thousand miles in the electronic age? He read Bartholomew Hanlon's article on the football team and Catholicism. It was a Tower of Pisa raised on a brick or two, tilted away from the neutral attitude Bartholomew affected. Parkman put through a call to South Bend.

"I wish you'd talked to me before writing that story, Bartholomew. I have learned the religious affiliations of the whole roster."

"The team can't talk to reporters."

"Well, you talked to two of them. You couldn't have made better choices."

A Methodist and a Muslim? No, Parkman meant their prowess at football. Wesley was the high scorer on the team, not unusual for kickers, and in a year when field goals outnumbered touchdowns, Wesley's numbers rose weekly. As for Natashi, "God only knows what the man could do if only we had a quarterback who could throw the ball. You wouldn't remember Biletnikoff."

"No," Bartholomew agreed.

"A legend. He could catch anything."

"A Catholic?"

"Ho ho. You know, I wouldn't be surprised. It doesn't matter, he played for Oakland."

However flawed, Bartholomew's article was a public introduction of the topic. What Parkman had learned was that the percentage of Catholics on the football team was lower than on the faculty.

"Wow."

"It doesn't mean much. What are they now but hired guns? It's like finding out that non-Catholics outnumber Catholics in maintenance, or on the grounds crew. Even so, it makes a strong rhetorical point."

After a distinguished career in the law and on the bench, Frank Parkman had looked forward to an indolent retirement, hours spent among the books he had acquired over the years, taking up again interests he had first acquired in college. He had not been a gung-ho alumnus of Notre Dame. He contributed, of course — given the persistence of the Notre Dame Foundation, it would have been difficult not to — but he was an infrequent presence at the Los Angeles Notre Dame Club. He had nothing against football or drinking but chose not to think that they alone were what bound him to his alma mater. Marie was dead now, and Frank's reading and the general nostalgia of his time of life turned his thoughts back to South Bend.

The Notre Dame Web site was a gaudy affair, and, of course, it purveyed the official view of what was going on. Parkman subscribed to the *Observer* and was startled at the editorial assumptions that guided the campus paper. Surely this was a minority view. Still, he talked with several kindred spirits, and some contacts were made with members of the board, without result. When several letters of inquiry, letters that had practically begged to be persuaded that things were not as they seemed on campus, went unanswered and unacknowledged, the Weeping Willow Society was formed. It now seemed undeniable that Notre Dame was on a dangerous path.

The only living, breathing contact Parkman and the society had at Notre Dame was Father Carmody.

"You've done well, Frank."

"Up to a point. What do *you* think of the

course Notre Dame is on?"

"I like the tone of your letters. Most letters to the administration are pretty strident."

"They haven't been answered."

"Because they are a rebuke, but one administered softly and thus more effectively."

"You think the administration knows they are going off the rails?"

"How could they not?"

"Surely you can influence them, Father."

"That was truer in the past than in the present."

"Any advice for us?"

"Keep it up. Think of the Berlin Wall. Think of the Soviet Union."

Parkman had thought of them on the flight back to the Coast. Apparently insuperable obstacles removed, a highly organized empire collapsing like a house of cards. Vivid indeed, but were they applicable to a Catholic university rushing headlong toward secularization?

When the body of Ignatius Willis was found on the practice putting green next to Rockne Memorial, there were members of the society who regarded this as a godsend. Parkman calmed them down.

163

"That is a tragedy, of course. We would be better advised to pray for the repose of his soul. What does it have to do with our interest?"

His view carried the day, as it had in the case of the trustee Francis O'Toole. Many had argued that O'Toole was their best bet on the board, but Parkman had opposed it.

"Why, Frank?"

"He was the dumbest one in our class."

"So why is he sitting on the board?"

"He has the Midas touch."

"Who was that girl he married?"

Parkman remained silent. No one else could remember Mimi. Parkman felt almost unfaithful to Marie for the way he still felt about her.

8

Larry Douglas read Grafton's account of the murder of Ignatius Willis with the same sinking depression he had felt when Jimmy Stewart took Laura up to the first tee and the ball washer there, leaving Larry ignominiously behind, guarding the corpus delicti. For him, it was axiomatic that Laura was a poor excuse for a cop. Her presence on campus security could only be explained as an exercise in affirmative action. She stayed on the job just to be close to Larry; she had admitted as much. Once, for a golden moment, the lovely Kimberley in Feeney the coroner's office had been smitten by him. He had recited poetry to her sighing delight; he had given her a peek into the depths and intricacies of the Douglas psyche. Ah, frailty, thy name is woman. She had succumbed to the blandishments of Henry Grabowski, who whispered French and Latin in her ear. Henry had left campus security and gone on to a position as watchman at a posh gated village in the northern suburbs.

"What exactly do you do?"

"Essentially nothing."

"Come on."

"I have an office in the gatehouse, and a small apartment there as well. The job consists of my *being* here. I sleep most of the day and then at nightfall make rounds. I have a flashing light on top of my golf mobile."

The pay, if you could believe Henry, always a matter of doubt, was half again as much as he had earned on campus security, and the benefits were incredibly generous.

"That is why I exercise maximum discretion in the matter of guests."

His eyes widened in a significant way. Was he referring to Kimberley?

Laura had repossessed Larry with a vengeance after his slight detour down the primrose path of dalliance. She considered them engaged, a plausible interpretation of the ring he had bought her.

"It's a friendship ring," he protested.

She dug him in the ribs. "Oh, you."

He had mocked her when she laid plastic over footprints on the edge of the green. Philip Knight had shared his interpretation of the action, if crossed eyes mean anything. But Phil had helped convoy Laura up to the first tee — she had a little trouble with even the slightest of grades — and there they had found other footprints to match those that Laura had covered with plastic on the green. It was her hour of triumph. She had eclipsed him. She had even earned a mention in Grafton's story. "An investigator with campus security, Laura Loftus . . ." Investigator! But the lowest moment of all had come when she hinted that she had done what she had done at the suggestion of her partner, Larry Douglas.

Condescended to by Laura! He considered taking a few days off. He considered looking for another job, some cushy spot like the one Henry Grabowski had found. No. That was not the Larry Douglas way. The only way to get beyond this terrible moment was to eclipse Laura, to make it clear that it was Larry Douglas who had the instincts of a cop. He must get his thoughts back on the murder of Iggie Willis.

"That is an inference," Feeney said. "What he died of was very likely self-applied."

"So your judgment is suicide."

Feeney was alarmed by so unequivocal an interpretation. "No, no. It goes the other way, too. Someone else might have poured all that liquor into him."

"It's got to be one or the other."

"That is not for me to decide. That is up to the police."

Larry caught just a glimpse of the lovely Kimberley in the next office. He raised his voice. "You're right, Doctor. I'll get right on it."

"I'm not deaf," Feeney complained.

Before leaving, Larry strode to the door of Kimberley's office. She was not there.

"Suspects?" Jimmy Stewart asked. "As far as I'm concerned, we've got a suicide here. Probably inadvertent."

"But the green towel," Larry pleaded.

"There are always unexplained things, Larry. You've got to learn to live with it."

"And the footprints?" It cost him much to bring this up.

"They don't mean anything as far as I can see."

A lesser man would have embraced this dismissal, perhaps eliciting as well some negative comments on Laura's enthusiasm. "I don't know. It looks as if the man who took the towel from the washer brought it down to the putting green."

"Did your girlfriend send you down here?"

"Girlfriend?"

"Okay, fiancée. When's the wedding?"

"Over my dead body."

"How many do you need?"

Grafton wore his hat as he sat at his desk. He greeted Larry with a look of benign condescension.

"Well, you did it, didn't you? It's the same old story."

Larry sat. "Okay, what did I do?"

"Got the thing all hushed up. I've been forbidden to write anymore about the death of Iggie Willis unless there are new developments. The power of Notre Dame."

"Don't look for any new developments."

"Oh, I know the local police are in your pocket."

"You made it sound like murder."

"Did I?" He pushed back his hat. Too far. It tumbled to the floor behind him. "Of course I did. That man had enemies."

"How so?"

"Surely you have checked out the Web site on which the dead man and others were excoriating the administration for not firing Weis."

"How would I get hold of it?"

Grafton, hatless, swung to his computer. His fingers danced on the keyoard. "There."

Larry had to come around the desk to see

the screen clearly: CheerCheerFor*Old*Notre-Dame.com. Grafton scrolled down so that Larry got a sense of the inflammatory entries on the site.

"Looks like he made a lot of friends."

Grafton swung his chair again, and Larry went back around the desk.

"Where there are friends, there are enemies. What proportion of the alumni do you think would agree with that Web site? A small, a very small percentage. That leaves the vast majority, many of whom might cheerfully have wrung his neck."

"Or filled him full of booze."

"A serious cop would investigate these things."

"So would a serious reporter."

Back in his car, Larry thought of Chita, the sassy little member of the cleanup crew who had found the body. No, she wanted to give that credit to Bridget. Only Bridget had been nowhere to be found. The wisest course seemed to be to go back to the very beginning and start over.

In his pad, he had noted Chita's name and address.

9

To Jimmy Stewart, Larry Douglas was both a rebuke and a pain in the whatchamacallit. The gung-ho kid from Notre Dame campus security reminded Jimmy of his own idealistic early days on the force, just back from the army, where his experience as an MP had been the open sesame. Law and order, right against wrong, the forces of peace and decency against the bad guys. Of course, the real world turned out not to be quite like that. There was a time when Jimmy might have gone over to the ostensible enemy, figuring what the hell. His wife had taken a powder; black and white were no longer vivid contrasts in South Bend. He had been saved from that by the appearance of Phil Knight on the local scene. Phil's brother, Roger, was a balloon of a man, apparently brilliant, who had been offered a lucrative position on the Notre Dame faculty and brought his private investigator brother along with him.

The funny thing was that Jimmy and Phil had come together when Phil had been activated to represent the interest of the University of Notre Dame, that is, to thwart the efforts of the South Bend police to get too curious about anything that had happened on campus. It seemed a situation guaranteed to make the two of them hate one another. Why hadn't that happened? Phil's rock-bottom integrity, mainly. He represented his client to the hilt, but there was no way that he was going to pretend that black was white or vice versa. He wasn't a hired gun. It was a refreshing reminder, and Jimmy had responded to it. They had become friends. Jimmy had almost got used to Roger, a special case if there ever was one.

Jimmy met Phil for coffee in a place out on 31. Not much talk at the outset, and then, "Jimmy, I don't like it."

"The coffee?"

"The body on the putting green."

"The suicide."

"Do you really believe that?"

"No."

"So let's get serious."

Getting serious involved checking out all the groups that had suddenly formed to raise hell on one basis or another. It turned out that Phil had more than an abstract interest. Roger was being harassed.

"They were waiting for him after class. His golf cart was festooned with toilet paper. A huge balloon had been attached to it. Do you know what they're calling him?"

"What?"

"The Goodyear Blimp."

"What brought this on?"

"His name appears on a list of supporters of the proposal to shut down Notre Dame football."

"Geez."

"He doesn't remember giving his consent. Apparently he didn't say no forcefully enough. Now he has become the poster boy for the outfit."

It was pretty clear that Phil did not like his little brother being made fun of. Ever since they had come to Notre Dame, Roger had been treated royally. Lots of enthusiastic students, teach anything he wanted, an ideal situation. The present situation was a complete reversal of that. Phil had gotten used to being told his brother was the best thing that had happened to Notre Dame in recent years. Now he was being made a figure of fun. The Goodyear Blimp!

"He taking it bad?"

"Jimmy, he thinks it's funny. You know Roger."

"I'm not sure I do."

"I know what you mean. He insists on keeping that replica of the blimp on his golf cart as he goes around campus."

"Can this hurt him?"

"That's his point. He is the Huneker Professor of Catholic Studies. For life. Jimmy, they pay him a bundle, I'll say no more."

"So why are you worried?"

"God damn it, he's my brother."

"He's not heavy, he's your brother?"

"No and yes."

That was good enough for Jimmy. So they called on Professor Lipschutz.

"You're Roger's brother?" Lipschutz said to Phil. "The man is a genius."

"People keep telling me that. He's also naive. He doesn't remember giving permission to add his name to your list."

"Oh, there's no doubt of that. Professor Bird was a witness."

"Professor Bird doesn't remember giving permission for his name to be used either."

"Have they asked that their names be withdrawn?"

This was the sticky point. Roger was

174

rather enjoying being pilloried in public, and Otto Bird had simply murmured, *"o tempora, o mores."*

"Cicero," Roger had explained.

As far as Phil was concerned, that was an unsavory suburb of Chicago.

"Ask them to remove your name, Roger," he had suggested.

"Phil, it's a tempest in a teapot," Roger had replied.

Which didn't give them a lot of clout with Lipschutz. He had been regarding Phil with a sad expression.

"You represent the university, don't you?"

"Don't you?"

"In a sense, yes, a quite disinterested sense. I want this institution to regain its soul."

"By dropping football?"

"That is only a start."

"Do you realize what they are doing to Roger? They're calling him the Goodyear Blimp."

"I know. He called to tell me that. He seemed exuberant about it."

"What exactly does your group have in mind? Other than having my brother made a fool of?"

"If I told you, you would alert your employers."

175

Father Carmody, it turned out, had a mole in the organization, Wessel.

"A good man, in his way. Simply has no appreciation for sports. It was a streak of idealism that made him susceptible to Lipschutz. I can understand that. Of course, Lipschutz's motives are complicated."

Lipschutz, Father Carmody told them, was badgering the administration to start a research center modeled on the Princeton Institute for Advanced Study, with himself as director.

"Grant him a few premises and it's not a bad idea. At least, no more wacky than a lot of others that have gained support in recent years. The man wants a sinecure."

"What's he got?"

Father Carmody explained the term.

"It is a feature of the modern university," he said sadly. "Everyone is out for number one. For Lipschutz, football is merely a target of opportunity."

10

Bartholomew Hanlon had the permissible thought that it was his interview with Professor Rimini that had given focus to the current campus rumblings. The professor had raised the question of the number of Catholics on the football team, and Bartholomew had gotten a good article out of that. The collapse of Notre Dame football had somehow seemed to give credence to the Weeping Willow Society's concerns about the drift of the university toward secularism. Raising the question of the number of Catholics on the faculty had doubtless been important, but to many it seemed abstract. Professors came one at a time and did not wear percentages on their foreheads. Besides, to friend and foe alike, while the problem could be stated in the present, the solution, if any, lay far off in a misty future. How many of us are truly worried about how the world will look in fifty years, seventy-five years? But to ask how many Catholics were on a football team that had amassed the worst record in the history of Notre Dame could focus the mind. And would this have been clarified if Bartholomew had not interviewed Professor Rimini? Or if he had not written the article about John Wesley and John Foster Natashi?

In order to keep the pot boiling, the interviewing went on.

"Oh, no you don't," Rimini said, when Bartholomew looked in the open door of his office.

"Is something wrong?"

"Wrong? Just because you made me sound like Fulton Sheen on a bad day? Half my non-Catholic colleagues think I'm on a crusade to run them off the reservation." He stopped to inhale. "Come in and close the door."

"Professor Rimini, if I misquoted you, we'll run a correction."

"Please, no. I mean it. I shouldn't have talked to you. It's my fault, I should have known better."

"That makes me look pretty bad."

The suggestion that zealots should ask how many Catholics are on the football team had not been a serious one, perhaps. Rimini had considered it the reductio ad absurdum of the efforts of the Weeping Willow Society. Now, to his alarm, he was being looked upon as the foremost agitator to rid the campus of non-Catholics.

"I've heard from the AAUP! Spurred on by people here, of course."

"What's the AAUP?"

"The American Association of University Professors. Not much of a threat, believe me. I'm a member. But I also got a call from the ACLU."

The representative of the ACLU said they were looking into the possibility that Rimini's activities fit under recent hate crime legislation.

"That's crazy, Professor. The article made it clear that you couldn't care less about the percentage of Catholics on the faculty."

"Of course it's clear. You don't think people actually read, do you? It was your headline that did it."

RIMINI RECALLS TEAM HUDDLE AT MASS. He had told Bartholomew of those early morning team Masses on game day. He said it with a sort of sneer, asking Bartholomew if he knew that God was Irish.

"Only on his mother's side."

Rimini had roared. "That's good. You ought to write."

His message now was *Don't write.*

179

"But surely if you're being harassed and threatened . . ."

"Did I say that? Did I use those words, harass, threaten?" He clamped his hand on his bald head, moving it around as if he were looking for the seams.

Rimini had liked the reference to his own years on the team, however.

"Were the players smaller then?"

"What do you mean?"

A knock on the door. Rimini shouted something, and the door opened to reveal a huge man. He dipped his head and came into the office.

"You've become famous," he said to Rimini.

"Here's the culprit. He wrote the story."

The large man nodded. "Lots of typos." He extended a large hand. "George Wintheiser."

"Don't talk to him," Rimini urged, half seriously. "He'll ruin your name."

"You played football," Bartholomew said. From an early age he had stuffed his memory with data on Notre Dame football. He had not fed this habit much of late, but those boyhood efforts had created a vast database of scores, statistics, honors, bowls.

"A little."

"A little!" Rimini said. "The MVP in the

Super Bowl!"

Bartholomew looked more closely at the man's large hands. On his right hand was unmistakably the NFL championship ring. On his left hand was his Notre Dame ring, which nearly concealed a plain gold band. Wintheiser took the easy chair, and Bartholomew remained in the chair across the desk from Rimini, an uncomfortable chair, doubtless to discourage students from long stays.

"Professor Rimini was telling me of the rough treatment he's been getting for recalling the religious practices of the team in his time."

"It was the same when I played," Wintheiser said.

"Were all the players Catholic?"

"Oh, no, but everyone came to those Masses."

"Was it required?"

Wintheiser looked at him. "No more than playing football in the first place."

"This is all off the record," Rimini said, when Bartholomew felt he should leave the two alumni alone.

"Bartholomew," Wintheiser said, "if I were you, I'd go after the critics of the team. What a comic crew."

"Not a bad idea." Not a particularly good

181

one either. The attack on Roger Knight had made him an even more sympathetic figure. Iggie Willis was dead. And Bartholomew had no desire to make fun of someone like Frank Parkman.

"M. Le Professeur, puis-je avoir une minute de votre temps?"

Guido Senzamacula jumped nervously. He turned with an agonized expression when Bartholomew, coming up behind him in a Decio hallway, made his foray into French.

"The object is not to fit French into English boxes, young man. The object is to speak French."

"I never had conversational French," Bartholomew said, following Senzamacula into his office. The professor closed the door.

"Good," he whispered. "If you want conversation, go to France. Even Quebec."

"Professor, I see that your name is on Professor Lipschutz's demand that Notre Dame abandon football."

"What?" He seemed genuinely surprised.

"It's been in all the papers, the student papers."

Senzamacula's hands lifted involuntarily as he looked at the ceiling. "Please. No offense, but I never read such papers."

"Well, anyway, here's your name."

Senzamacula took the paper and read with visible horror. "Ban football? Me? What would Piero say?"

"Piero?"

"My son. Television."

Senzamacula dropped into his desk chair like an unopened parachute. He stared at Bartholomew but apparently did not see him. The saga of his son Piero, born at Notre Dame, educated at Notre Dame, Notre Dame through and through, from the top of his headphones to the soles of his workaday sneakers, followed.

"What does he do?"

"He televises games. He doesn't work the camera anymore. He's in the truck, directing it all."

"Notre Dame games."

"All of them. He tells me he has not missed a game since he graduated. That sounds impossible. Like Father Hesburgh saying he has said Mass every day since his ordination, no matter where he happened to be, Moscow, the South Pole, wherever. I'm sure it's true, though."

"Professor, you are absolutely certain you did not give Professor Lipschutz permission to put your name on that list?"

Senzamacula actually lifted his hand. "As

God is my judge."

Again he picked up the paper Bartholomew had given him. "Bird! Knight! I can't believe that they signed this petition."

It seemed another and related story.

Lipschutz was in his hideaway office in Brownson behind Sacred Heart, one of a string of offices that looked out on a parking lot. Bartholomew had wheedled the location from the secretary of Lipschutz's department.

"Yes, yes, come in."

Lipschutz was moving around the office, shifting books from one surface to another; there were piles of manuscripts on the desk. His computer was aglow.

"I have to correct proofs for three books at the same time." His eyes grazed over Bartholomew. "I have been asked to lecture in Berlin in the spring." He pointed to the wall. "Those are my honorary degrees."

"I hate to interrupt . . ."

"Nonsense, nonsense. Sit down. That document in the gold frame? A tribute from the Swiss government. I am currently at work on four different volumes."

"Amazing."

"I also work at home. Young man, you see before you a specimen of the much discussed but seldom beheld research professor."

Lipschutz's reddish hair was cut in a sort of military style, his beard clipped; he was lean, and his belt was high above his hips, cinching his narrow waist. There was a gap of inches between his shoes and the bottoms of his pants. He had all the nervousness of a sparrow with bluebirds in the vicinity, his head looking now here, now there, now everywhere.

"A suggestion, young man." He paused. "What is your name?"

"Bartholomew Hanlon."

"Interesting. Bartholomew, your story should emphasize the positive. The university is striving for excellence? Good. It wants to achieve status as a research university? Better. But those are words, phrases. It must be made concrete. Personal."

He waited for Bartholomew to grasp his point.

"I think you should concentrate on a living, breathing research professor. Describe his day, his projects, his achievements."

Bartholomew glanced at the wall. "An excellent idea."

"I will tell you everything you need to know. I have offprints of articles. I could give you some of those." His tone was reluctant. "My books, of course, are in the library."

"Professor Guido Senzamacula says he did not give you permission to put his name on your petition to abandon football."

"Nonsense. Of course he did." Rows of very even teeth were revealed in a smile reminiscent of Teddy Roosevelt's. "You have heard of the absentminded professor?"

"He was surprised to see the names of Otto Bird and Roger Knight on the petition."

"I secured those myself."

"They're making fun of Roger Knight, you know."

"I know, I know. They killed Socrates."

Lipschutz was less forthcoming when asked about the demonstration his group allegedly planned.

"A mere means. To get their attention. The administration has to understand that I am the best friend they have."

"Have you made that point to them?"

"They can't possibly not know it."

He gave Bartholomew an offprint of one of his articles, "There Are No Rights in Roman Law," assuring him that he would give the press every help he could.

Setting off to see Roger Knight, it occurred to Bartholomew that it would be at least as easy to caricature and lampoon Lipschutz as it was Roger Knight. The Goodyear Blimp. Despite his love for Roger Knight, Bartholomew smiled.

11

He canceled his classes. He couldn't sleep.
He longed to talk to Piero and yet he
avoided him. Every day he had gone to
Cedar Grove to visit the grave of his wife
and son, consulting them to find out what
he could do to convince Piero that he had
not signed Lipschutz's abominable petition.

"Dad, I believe you. Calm down."

"I want you to forgive me!"

"All right, I forgive you."

Words. Of course Piero would say what he
asked him to say. He was a good son, a son
he had betrayed. In Cedar Grove he had
the distinct feeling that Jessica agreed.

What must the administration think of
him? Guido Senzamacula had brought with
him from the Old World the unformulated
conviction that superiors are superiors,
bosses are bosses. Tenure? Did anyone really
believe that the university wouldn't be able
to get rid of a rebellious professor? His

phone kept ringing, and he let it ring. Piero had insisted that he have caller ID, and he knew it was the ineffable Lipschutz calling to badger him. Piero came by at least once a day. He was staying in a motel with his crew; so much for the hope that he would make use of his old room.

"Dad, get out of the house. Teach your classes. You're cracking up."

Was he? Sometimes he thought that for years he had been waiting for such an occasion, that he longed to just let go and drift away, into sleep, retirement, even death.

"It won't be long," he whispered over the graves in Cedar Grove.

To die, to sleep. Not even music soothed his tortured breast. The Mozart concertos he loved now seemed only to jangle his nerves. One night, under cover of darkness, he crept across campus to Decio, let himself in, and sat in his office with the lights out. It was ridiculous. He knew it was ridiculous. He knew Piero was concerned about him. But he could not wish away the thought that after so many happy years at Notre Dame he had allowed Lipschutz to make a pariah of him.

He could make a statement, publicly declare that his name had been used without his permission. No one would believe him.

189

It would be his word against that of the eloquent Lipschutz. His colleague infuriated him by dismissing Guido's claim that he had not signed the petition to remove football once and forever from Notre Dame. What was Notre Dame without football? That could be the opening sentence of his declaration, letting the administration know he was on their side. The game that Guido did not understand, that he personally cared nothing for, loomed now as large on the horizon of his mind as the golden dome. He should have made an effort to like football. Out of loyalty to the university. To be on even better terms with Piero. Like a remorseful penitent, he promised God that he would attend every home game for the rest of his life.

A knock on his office door. It was eleven o'clock at night. Who could know he was here? He had not turned on the lights. He sat frozen in his chair.

"Professor? Are you in there?"

Not Lipschutz. Not Piero.

He turned on the lights before he opened the door and looked, blinking, at the uniformed man.

"You're Professor Senzamacula."

Was this an arrest? Guido nodded.

"Your son asked me to check to see if you

were here."

"Yes, yes, I'm here."

The guard looked at Guido's desk. "Your phone's off the hook. He's been trying to reach you."

Guido hurried to the desk and replaced the phone. What had he been thinking when he laid the receiver on the desk?

"You all right, Professor?"

"Of course, of course. What's your name?"

"Larry Douglas."

Guido tried to laugh. The name was on a patch sewn to the young man's shirt. He pointed to it, as if he had been making a joke.

"You going to stay here, Professor? It's pretty late."

"A little longer, yes."

"I could take you home."

"Oh, I can walk."

Larry Douglas was looking at his feet. Slippers, but doubtless it was the robe and pajamas that surprised him more. Guido had not taken into account how he was dressed when he set out for campus.

"Perhaps you should see me home."

On the way there, bumping along in the odd little vehicle the guard drove, Guido looked at the great disc of the moon. The

mad were once called lunatics. Was he going mad?

12

Chita didn't recognize Larry Douglas at first, and he wished he'd been wearing his uniform. Her eyes narrowed suspiciously as he reminded her of how they had met. Then, like two black olives, her eyes glistened. She dug him in the ribs.

"Backseat Charlie."

"Larry."

"So how did you find me?"

"Look, I'm a cop."

"Campus security makes you a cop?"

Larry didn't want to go into that, not with this sassy little dish. How shapely and compact Chita seemed compared to Laura, but who wouldn't?

Chita was the cashier at the first window that cars going through the McDonald's drive-through stopped at. Finding her had just been lucky. At Personnel, they were surprised when he asked for the names of those on the postgame cleanup crew.

"But they're temporaries."

"There must be regulars."

"They're not regular employees."

"Thanks for your help."

"Have a nice day."

Gaboriau, in charge of grounds, had a little office in the low building north of the Credit Union, and Larry found him in the huge shed filled wih mowers, pickups, all kinds of vehicles. He kept walking around while Larry talked.

"Come around on Friday afternoon, kid. That's when I hire."

"Geez, I'm not looking for a job. I've got a job."

Gaboriau turned and looked at the uniform. "I noticed. Everyone I hire for that crew has another job."

"Weekends are big in campus security." Larry could have wept at being thought a candidate for the campus cleanup crew.

"I'm trying to locate a member of that crew. The crew that found the body on the putting green. I interrogated some of them." Well, one of them. "A woman named Chita."

"Oh, geez."

"You remember her?"

"She's a regular."

"How can I locate her?"

Gaboriau leered. "It would be a waste of time. I'll say no more."

This angered Larry more than the suggestion that he had come here seeking employment on the cleanup crew, probably because he knew he just wanted to see Chita again.

"You interrogated her?" Gaboriau asked. "Didn't you get her address then?"

"You can't help me?"

The address Chita had given him was a McDonald's. When he had looked it up, he could imagine her laughing at him. After talking with Gaboriau, the idiot in maintenance, he went back to the McDonald's and went inside. He was hungry. It was while he was waiting in line that he spotted her at the cashier's window of the drive-through. He ordered large fries and a Coke and sat where he could watch Chita. Sooner or later, she had to get a break. When she did, she came around the counter with a drink and collapsed in a plastic seat. Larry went and sat across from her. It took a minute before she said, "Backseat Charlie."

"I was up front."

"So what do you want?"

"When do you get off?"

"Someone's picking me up."

"This is official. I want to talk to you."

"We're talking now."

"You mentioned a woman, a fellow crew member, named Bridget."

"That's who's picking me up."

"What time?"

"When I get off."

Larry waited.

"At six."

That gave him several hours. For no good reason that he could think of, he went home and put on his uniform. Who doesn't look better in a uniform? He was back at the McDonald's at five thirty, parked where he could keep an eye on both side entrances. It was ten after six when Chita came out, still wearing her work clothes. She looked around and then came right across the parking lot to Larry's car. Only it was the car next to his she was headed for. There was an older woman behind the wheel. Larry hopped out. The woman behind the wheel dipped down to get a better look, and her mouth dropped open. Chita had opened the passenger door.

"You told!" she cried.

"This is Larry. You remember him, Bridget."

Larry said, "I want to have a few words with you, ma'am."

"Get in the backseat, Charlie."

Larry got in the backseat. Bridget sat now with her back rammed back into the seat, staring straight ahead.

"Bridget, I haven't told him a thing."

"Sure."

"What hasn't she told me, Bridget?"

"This solves your problem," Chita said. "Just give them to good old Larry. He's a cop."

Bridget popped the trunk open, got out, went back there, and a moment later pulled open the back door and tossed a plastic bag at Larry. Bridget was behind the wheel and Chita hanging over the front seat when Larry opened the plastic bag and saw a huge pair of shoes. Strombergs.

"Where'd you get these?"

Bridget had found the shoes in a trash barrel up the mall toward O'Shaughnessy. After they made a grand sweep of the mall, they gathered up the trash barrels and threw them onto the truck. The shoes were visible when Bridget began to pick up the barrel they were in. She fished them out, looked around, and then hid them behind some bushes in front of the dining hall. Later she came back for them.

"Good work, Bridget."

She just looked at him in the rearview mirror. "Keep my name out of it."

197

He tossed the plastic bag into his trunk and drove away.

13

Father Neil Genoux, special advisor to the president, had long felt that the Main Building was morally under siege, but only the ineffable Lipschutz actually brought his campaign physically to the doors of the building. Maisie, Genoux's secretary, had alerted him to the presence of a motley crew at the bottom of the stairs leading to the entrance of the Main Building.

"They demand to see the president."

"Which group is it?"

"Lipschutz."

It was a name that lent itself to disdainful pronunciation, no doubt of that, but did even Maisie know what lay behind Lipschutz's demands? Genoux was not alone in thinking that, if the university agreed to open a new and vast research center with Lipschutz in charge, not another word would be heard from him about the abomination of Notre Dame football. It was blackmail, pure and simple.

At any other time, the man might simply be ignored. Now, his appearance outside seemed to presage wave after wave of groups intent on making life miserable for the administration. The Web site founded by the unfortunate Ignatius Willis continued to heap criticism on the coach and on those who had hired him. The Weeping Willow Society, while more sedate and rational, continued to bombard the Main Building with embarrassing inquiries. And now there was the investigation into how many Catholics were on the football team! The suggestion seemed to be that it was having heretics in uniform that explained the string of losses suffered by the team. The danger was that, if Lipschutz was ignored, he would be back daily until he was noticed; and, if he was not ignored, the precedent might bring other angry hordes to their doorstep. At the same time, the formidable George Wintheiser, joined now by Rimini, the economist, was demanding the administration come vocally to the support of the coach and team. Genoux telephoned Father Carmody.

"Send someone for me," the old priest said, when Genoux had explained the situation. There was the promise of battle in Carmody's voice. If only Genoux could turn the matter over to the older priest. He asked Maisie to pick up Father Carmody at Holy Cross House and bring him here.

"Not by the main entrance."

Maisie just looked at him. Well, it had been a dumb remark.

Half an hour later, Father Carmody sauntered into Genoux's office with a cigarette smoldering in his hand. "Where can I put this out?"

"Anywhere. Here, I'll take it." Smoking in the Main Building! Perhaps it had been a mistake to enlist Carmody. He took the cigarette and tossed it into the wastebasket.

The older priest began to tell of the way Ted Hesburgh had handled protesters years ago. "He confronted them face-to-face, told them they had ten minutes to disperse or they were out on their ear. That was the end of that. Force can only be met by forcefulness."

"You want me to go out there and confront them?"

"Of course not. You're too young. This requires gravitas. I'll go."

Too young? Gravitas? Genoux was older than the president. But it was Carmody's offer to confront Lipschutz himself that balanced any pique Genoux might have felt.

"I could go with you."

Carmody thought about it. "Only if you keep in the background."

Dismissing the suggestion of the elevator, Carmody marched down the wide ancient steps of the building, up and down which he had gone many times over the years. The present trouble seemed to put spring in his step. His shoulders were back, his arms moved in a military rhythm. Along the first floor corridor, then, lined with Gregori's paintings that Genoux had never managed to like, to the closed double doors. Carmody stepped back and nodded, indicating that Genoux should open them. And then, through those opened doors, Charles Carmody strode out to meet the foe. Genoux sidled out and, following instructions, kept in the background.

The scene at the foot of the stairs was not at first frightening. There seemed as many curious students as signers of Lipschutz's petition, but the sparseness of the crowd seemed made up for by the idiot who kept banging on a drum. There were banners. SOCCER, NOT FOOTBALL; others wondering why there was not a women's football team. And, dear God, a television crew.

Carmody took up his stance at the top of the stairs, legs apart, hands behind him. He waited. Lipschutz made a gesture and the drum stopped beating. Something like silence fell.

"Where is the president?" Lipschutz asked querulously.

For answer, Carmody put out his hand and, with his index finger, motioned to Lipschutz to mount the stairs.

Lipschutz looked undecided. Someone whispered in his ear. He looked up at Father Carmody and then began to come up the stairs.

As he grew closer, he noticed Genoux. "We can discuss this," he said pleadingly.

Father Carmody held out his hand for the document Lipschutz ws carrying.

"There are many points of view on this proposal," Lipschutz said, addressing Genoux, who moved farther into the background.

Carmody's imperious hand was still thrust out to Lipschutz. The television crew was creeping up the steps, recording it all. Finally, Lipschutz held out the document. Carmody took it with a sweep of his hand.

"You must take it to the president. To the board."

For answer, Father Carmody tore the document, first in two, then again, almost a third time. Unsuccessfully. Then he flung the pieces in Lipschutz's face. Unaccountably, a cheer went up from below.

"Come, Father," Father Carmody said, and in a moment they were inside the closed doors.

"That ought to do it. Thanks for your help."

When they got back to Genoux's office, the fire in his wastebasket had been put out.

Who would have thought that in the present university climate such a gesture as Carmody's would be cheered? Later, on the evening news, Genoux watched the old fellow as he stood statuesque at the top of the stairs, the grand gesture commanding Lipschutz to come to him, the even grander gesture of tearing up the document and tossing the pieces in Lipschutz's face. The camera had then turned to show the cheering throng at the foot of the stairs. The drum had started up again. In the distance, a band of elderly men approached. Force of a kind had been met with forcefulness of a rare kind.

14

A wide-awake Notre Dame alumnus in the sales department arranged to have several hundred miniature Goodyear Blimps, inflatable balloons, sent to Roger Knight, who distributed them to his class and to anyone else he ran into. Bartholomew Hanlon blew up the one he had been given and looked at it sadly.

"Did you actually sign that statement, Professor?"

"No."

"And Otto Bird?"

"No more than I did."

"But Lipschutz insists that you did."

"*Quidquid recipitur,* Bartholomew. *Quidquid recipitur.* We hear what we want to hear."

"You have to ask for a retraction."

"Do I? Whatever for? It is not the first time that what I have said has been misunderstood."

Phil was not as philosophical as Roger

about the teasing his brother was getting, particularly because it was based on the false premise that he subscribed to Lipschutz's quixotic campaign to rid Notre Dame of football.

Otto Bird regarded it with the same amusement as Roger. "Of course, no one is likening me to a blimp."

"You lack the qualifications," Roger said with a smile.

"It will die down," Otto said. "Everything eventually does."

It might have been a melancholy remark, but that was not Otto's style. At ninety-three he still got up every day with the optimism that had been with him all his life. Another day, things to do, so do them, don't worry that nightfall is inevitable.

So, despite Phil's protests and those of Bartholomew Hanlon and other students, Roger floated above the controversy as a metaphorical blimp. That became more difficult when Phil brought him Piero Macklin, a member of the television crew that had brought the Boston College game to a startled nation. Peter had stayed on.

"My father lives here."

"Here meaning Notre Dame?"

"Guido Senzamacula."

"My dear friend. But your name?"

"A professional elision. How would Piero Senzamacula look among the credits?"

"Refreshing."

"My father is all broken up about being linked with this campaign to eliminate football. He thinks I think he really is involved."

"Names got on the list of sponsors in strange ways, Piero."

"Including yours?"

"Including mine."

"What are you going to do about it?"

"Pretty much what I have been doing."

"Which is?"

"Nothing."

"I wish my father could take it so lightly. He talks about nothing else. Would you come with me to talk with Lipschutz?"

"I don't think it would do any good."

"It would do me a lot of good. He has to understand how my father is taking this. He reacts to things in an exaggerated way. He is a rock-bottom loyalist so far as Notre Dame goes. The idea that he would campaign in a public way against something so connected with the university as football is unthinkable."

"He is too upset to talk to Lipschutz himself?"

"I couldn't put him through that. He can't

bear the sound of the man's name."

Roger knew the location of Lipschutz's office because it was located near his own in Brownson Hall. For Roger, apart from isolation from other faculty offices, the attraction had been the adjacent parking lot where he could leave his golf cart and get to his office without running the gamut of stairs. They were in the little hallway off which his own office and Lipschutz's hideaway opened when there was a commotion behind them. Soon a distraught Lipschutz appeared. He looked wildly at Roger.

"We have been insulted! Publicly insulted."

"The Goodyear Blimp business? I consider that almost praise."

Lipschutz angrily dismissed this. He began to pick pieces of paper from his clothing. He had yet to take any notice of Piero.

Lipschutz had trouble with the key to his office, but finally he got it open and went raging inside, giving an incoherent tale of a confrontation on the steps of the main building. At his desk, he turned to Roger and there were actual tears in his eyes. "He tore it up!"

"Your petition?"

"And they cheered. It was like *Patton,* only

all wrong." His expression was desolate.

"Then it's over," Roger said.

"Over! Over!" Lipschutz was transformed by the suggestion. "Never. Now it is a battle to the death. I will humble them, I promise you. I will get the last laugh. They will eat their horses before I am done with them."

"Horst, you've made your point."

Lipschutz's expression was almost of contempt. "You don't understand."

"The research center?"

"How did you know of that?"

"Is it a secret? I think Father Carmody mentioned it."

"Carmody! He was their henchman. He tore up the petition."

Roger could not wait to get Father Carmody's account of what had happened on the steps of the Main Building. Suddenly, Piero moved to Lipschutz, grabbed the lapels of his jacket, and pulled him close.

"You drop that goddamn petition or I'll beat the shit out of you." Piero spoke with a controlled rage, if not with the vocabulary Lipschutz was accustomed to.

"Who are you?" Horst's terrified eyes rolled to Roger. "Who is this maniac?"

Piero gave him a thorough shaking, then pushed him into the desk chair, which began to roll toward the wall, with the astounded Lipschutz looking at his assailant.

"My name is Senzamacula. Get out a sheet of paper. I want you to write that my father has never had anything to do with your stupid petition."

"Roger," Lipschutz yelped.

"Come, Piero," Roger suggested. "I think you have made your point."

Piero hesitated. The phone rang. It was Phil, calling to tell Roger what he and Jimmy had been doing.

Roger turned away, and told Phil about Piero's attack.

"I'm surprised it wasn't Wintheiser."

Roger hung up and turned toward Piero. His face was still flushed with anger and his body tense. He was half the size of Wintheiser. Roger managed to get Piero out the door.

Settled in the golf cart, Piero said, "I could have killed the sonofabitch."

15

There are levels of hell, and Professor Horst Lipschutz had descended through several of them in a single day. In retrospect, it seemed to him that he had been taken to the pinnacle of the Main Building and told that he could be master of all he surveyed. It had long rankled him that the administration was impervious to his suggestion for a research center, a real research center, that could justify the university's claims for itself. No one who had spent as much time in academic circles as he could really be surprised by the density and irrationality of his colleagues, nor did he by any means confine this assessment to the administration. The faculty were, if possible, worse. Imagine the reaction of Guido Senzamacula to the generous move that Lipschutz had made, adding him to the signatories of his petition, admittedly anticipating his agreement, but how could any rational animal disagree? That Otto Bird and Roger Knight denied that they had given him permission to include their names had been a disappointment, of course, but they had not made any public protest.

Of course, it was not the inclusion of other names on the petition that mattered. No need for false modesty. It was the first name, that of Horst Lipschutz that should have brought home to the administration the decision they faced. Had he ever seriously thought that he could persuade the university to drop football? Actually, he had. From the beginning, though, that had been a mere target of opportunity. Whether or not they saw reason on that matter was secondary; the essential thing was that, prompted in this way, they should finally concede the wisdom of entrusting the university's reputation as a research institution to his capable hands. Dear God, he had three books in the press at this very moment. His list of publications exceeded, he was sure, that of any other member of the faculty, and not merely in quantity. His was an international reputation. Had he not been honored by the Bavarian Academy?

To review his credentials now on this ignominious day was more than a justification for the tears that poured down his leathery cheeks, through the runnels that descended from either side of his nose to the corners of his mouth. A mouth whose lower lip trembled as he wept. Never in his worst nightmares had he been treated like this.

He tried unsuccessfully to eradicate from his mind the fiasco on the front steps of the administration building. How confidently he had marched there surrounded by a handful of representative supporters, his pace matching the beat of the drum that someone he did not recognize had thought to bring along. It was the drum that had made their presence one that could not be ignored. Finally, the doors of the entrance had opened, and Lipschutz took a deep breath. His moment of triumph was at hand. St. George Patton, pray for us. If he had known then what lay ahead . . .

He put his head on his desk and sobbed. His mistake had been to respond to that crooked finger of the evil little silver-haired priest who stood where the president should have been standing. Someone had whispered in his ear that this was Father Carmody, a power behind the scenes. An intermediary, nonetheless. He should have refused. He should have sent some lieutenant up those stairs. He should have . . .

Against his closed lids he could see again that dreadful priest tearing up his petition, tearing it again and again, disdainfully, and then flinging the pieces at him! It was the cheering and applause that accompanied this act that undid Lipschutz. He turned in confusion to what he had imagined were his supporters and other well-wishers. They were cheering, applauding, that abominable act. Then, as he stumbled down the stairs, brushing past the television, they began to laugh!

How in the name of God had he managed to get to his hideaway office, only a short distance from the scene of his ignominy? Ah, but his descent into hell was far from over. There was Roger Knight with some brute of a companion come to manhandle him.

Senzamacula! No doubt the coward had sent his muscular son to attack a colleague, to shake him as a terrier might shake a rat, to push him into his chair, which continued backward until his head hit the wall. Could there be anything worse than this day, in this life or the next?

Night fell and he remained in the office. He did not turn on the lights. The door was locked, of course, but what protection was a locked door against the forces of unreason? He grew hungry. He had to go to the bathroom. He did not dare. Only when he could bear the twin pains no longer did he unlock the door and look out. The men's room was at the end of the hall. There was a little alcove where machines delivered tasteless snacks for exorbitant prices. First things first. He went swiftly to the men's room. Inside, he hesitated before turning on the light. Nonsense. Still, he hid himself in a stall while he did his business. He could lift his feet from the floor if anyone intruded.

Relieved in several senses, he came out of the men's room. He was pondering the selections the machines offered when there was a sound behind him. An office door was opening. Lipschutz froze. At the sight of Roger Knight in the open door, Lipschutz cried out.

"Fear not, Horst. I am alone."

"That maniac attacked me. You were a witness."

"I want you to come with me. We don't want any repetition."

"You think he will be back?"

"Maybe someone else. I'll take you where you'll be safe."

Safe! Lipschutz could have cried out at all the word represented. "What did you mean, someone else?"

"Later. Let's go."

Some minutes later, he accompanied his enormous colleague to his waiting golf cart.

"Where are we going, Roger?"

"Holy Cross House."

PART THREE

1

Jimmy Stewart concluded that the presence of those matching shoe prints, some on the putting green, others up at the first tee where the towel was missing from the ball washer, might not prove that Willis had been killed, but they sure as hell meant that he had not died alone. Some guy with big feet had been there and for some oddball reason had stuffed the towel from the ball washer into Willis's mouth. Before or after he died, who knew? Phil Knight said that asking Feeney was like consulting the Delphic Oracle.

"The what?"

"Ask Roger."

"First chance I get. What size shoe do you wear?"

"Eleven."

"I wear a ten and I think I have big feet. Those prints were made by at least a fourteen."

This exchange took place before Grafton began to write about the Cinderella Fella, his fanciful story accompanied by a photograph of one of those footprints. Alongside it was a scale indicating the size of the shoe, which was at least a fourteen.

"He died under the eyes of God," Grafton had written piously, "but there was another pair of eyes as well, human eyes. In those small hours of that Sunday morning less than a week ago when, on the practice putting green of the Notre Dame golf course, Ignatius Willis went to meet his Maker. There was a human witness. He left his mark upon the greensward. (See accompanying photo.) And what happened there doubtless has left its mark on him."

He was reading these lines, half aloud, half from memory, when Larry Douglas entered his office.

"Have you read my story?"

"That's why I'm here. Who took the picture?"

"I did."

"What a great idea."

"Without my words, it's only a picture."

"Where can I get a copy?"

"Buy a paper."

"I mean a clearer one. The original."

Grafton took a small camera from his desk, turned it on, punched a button, and handed it to Larry. The young man from Notre Dame security studied it intently. "This is much clearer."

"We're not a magazine, Larry. We use newsprint."

"I think you and I are the only ones who still think something bad went on out there."

Grafton nodded. "The police act as if you hadn't drawn their attention to those shoe prints."

Larry's intent look became desolate. "That was my partner."

"Your fiancée?"

"Don't say that!"

"You've broken up with her?"

"It's a long story."

"It always is," Grafton said wearily, as if from experience. Only monks had less experience of women than he.

"Let me take this and have a print made."

"Larry, that camera is a tool of my trade."

"There's a drugstore up the street where I can do it. I'll have it back to you in ten minutes."

Grafton made a dismissive gesture, and Larry scooted from the office. Grafton was almost sorry he'd had the idea of accompanying his story with a photograph of that

221

shoe print. It was distracting. How could the reader savor his prose with that huge picture competing for his attention? The ratio between words and picture suddenly seemed far more than a thousand.

When the picture curled from the printer, Larry held his breath. Then he held the print for a full minute before he began to study it. Ever since Laura had drawn attention to shoe prints on the putting green, which had then been matched by identical ones at the ball washer, Larry had been dreaming of a way to turn her coup into his own. The sight of the photo next to Grafton's story had given him an idea. At the time, he was seated on the edge of his bed, bedraggled, unrested, looking at his shoes lying on their sides on the floor just out of reach.

"Larry, you don't work today."

He ignored Laura. His hand went out and grasped his shoe. He turned it over and studied its sole.

"Larry?"

"Go to sleep."

"Well, thanks a heap." She rolled onto her side, causing the waterbed to ripple, and pulled the blanket over her shoulder.

It wasn't that he was ignoring her. He

hadn't heard her. He stumbled across the room to the early bird edition he had bought at some godawful hour the night before. Asking Laura in was the line of least resistance. He did not want to make the long drive to where she lived. There he would have had to park and grapple for half an hour before she let him go and went inside. The last thing he remembered before falling asleep was her grumbling, "I hate waterbeds."

All through the night, his subconscious had apparently been at work. When he sat on the edge of the bed, his eye had been drawn fatefully to his shoe, to its sole, to the mark in the curve where sole met heel. Now, in the drugstore, he peered closely at the color print of Grafton's photo. He could have cried out. A diamond, a word beneath it. He would need a magnifying glass to make it out. No, no, he could read it. Stromberg! The same brand as the shoes that Bridget Sokolowski had turned over to him.

"Thanks," he said to Grafton, putting the camera on his desk.

"Let me see it."

The reporter took the print and held it some distance from his eyes. He nodded. "Of course it's clearer, and color helps."

He handed it back, and Larry began to breathe again. What would he have done if Grafton had noticed the trademark on the sole of the shoe? They could have formed a team. Perhaps a time for that would come, but for the moment it was Larry Douglas alone. Rather than go back to his room and Laura, he headed for campus security, where he could use a telephone.

None of the shoe stores in the area carried Stromberg shoes. Larry was disappointed but not discouraged. He pulled up Stromberg on the Internet. A Massachusetts firm. A number, but not an 800 number. Larry dialed it anyway.

"I'm calling from South Bend, Indiana. Where is the nearest outlet for your shoes?"

"Outlet? Retail outlet?"

"Shoe store."

"My dear fellow, Stromberg shoes are custom made."

"Each customer orders his own?"

"Our feet are our chief contact with the world," the voice went on. "Feet are not to be trifled with, feet . . ."

Larry hung up. There was no point in asking that fruitcake if he would tell Larry who his customers were. That could come later, after he matched the shoes Bridget had given him with the prints on the putting

224

green.

"I wonder," Grafton said, when Larry went back to the reporter's office to enlist his help. There seemed no point now in keeping his big inspiration a secret. "There must be a way."

"I could go around looking for people with big feet and ask them to show me the bottom of their shoes."

"The Cinderella Fella." Grafton smiled, in approval of the phrase he had had to fight with the editor to have above his story about the prints. "I wonder what would happen if I mentioned the make of the shoes in another story."

The little leap of hope in Grafton's voice reminded Larry of the eagerness with which he had rushed off to the drugstore to make that print.

"Who knows?"

It was when he was outside again, at his car, that he remembered that he still had the plastic bag in his trunk. He drove to a parking place by the St. Joseph River where he and Laura had spent hours he would rather not think about. After turning off the engine, he reached down, depressed the button to open the trunk, and got out. He reached into the bag and brought out a huge shoe and turned it over. Stromberg but nothing more. He was about to put it away again when it occurred to him to examine it further. The name was etched into the inside of the shoe. George Wintheiser.

2

Phil had been with Jimmy Stewart when the call from Father Genoux came. Jimmy's eyebrows shot up, and he handed the phone to Phil. "It's for you."

"Philip Knight?"

"Yes."

"Father Genoux. We've met."

"Yes."

"I was told I might find you there."

"What is it, Father?"

"I wonder if you've heard of the demonstration at the Main Building yesterday."

"I saw it on television."

"I know, I know. In any case, I received a call saying that Professor Lipschutz is missing. He can't be found. No one knows where he is. After what happened yesterday, you can imagine . . ."

"I'll be right there, Father."

"Father Carmody tells me that he has

227

retained your services, on behalf of the university."

"That's right."

"Whatever you can do, Mr. Knight. There's no need to come here. I will be anxious to hear what you may find out."

"Lipschutz," Phil said to Jimmy, when he had put down the phone. "He's missing."

"He's been all over television."

"He's not on campus, he's not at his home."

"They want you to find him?"

"I think they fear he might harm himself."

Alone on a slow day, Jimmy went across the street for lunch, a hamburger and a beer. He read Grafton's story about the Cinderella Fella and saw the photo of the shoe print. The guy must be a giant. Jimmy's eyes lifted from the paper. He stared at the winking name of a beer in neon in the window of the bar. Products have brands. Shoes are products.

He finished his lunch and went up the street to the paper.

"Great minds," Grafton purred. "The shoe is a Stromberg."

"Never heard of it."

"They're custom made."

"Where?"

"Massachusetts. They have a Web site."

Everybody had a Web site, even the South Bend police. Jimmy had never brought it up on his computer.

Back in his office, he decided he would tell Phil Knight about the Stromberg brand. His phone rang, and he wasn't surprised to find that it was Phil.

"Phil, I have something to tell you. Maybe important."

"Jimmy, Roger isn't here."

"What do you mean?"

"I thought he had gone to class. I don't think his bed has been slept in. His golf cart is missing, too."

"I'll be right there."

3

"We got there too late," Bingham lamented.

"How *did* you get there?"

"We walked."

"No wonder."

"It was all on television."

"We had signs," Potts said, having got the drift of the conversation. "SAVE OUR CLUB."

"Old Carmody would have torn that up, too."

"I thought he was retired."

"Retired, not dead."

"I know the distinction."

"They had to bring him back," Armitage Shanks said, in the tones of an insider. "These young pups can't handle anything."

"Do you approve of the humiliation of a colleague?"

"When it's self-administered."

What had happened on the steps of the Main Building the previous day might have been unknown by most and forgotten by the few who had witnessed it had not the local television station played the film made of the occasion over and over and over. By the magic of television, it loomed as large as another lost football game. Of course, the station could now justify this repetition because of the disappearance of Lipschutz.

"They should drag the lakes," Horvath advised.

"My wife reported me missing once."

"Missing what?"

"I had gone to Chicago, on impulse. Got caught in a snowstorm coming through Michigan City. Slid off the road and spent the night there."

"So you *were* missing."

"I was gone, not missing."

The others left Potts to his memories. Who would report any of them missing if they failed to show up someday?

"Whatever happened to the guy they found on the putting green?"

"I suppose they buried him."

"Was he killed or what?"

"What," said Potts, and it didn't seem to be a question.

"Potts is right. The verdict was suicide."

"Have they looked for Lipschutz on the golf course?"

"They should check the ball washers for

missing towels."

Debbie, the hostess, was scooting by, but Shanks caught her attention by catching her arm. Stopped abruptly, she teetered, then fell onto his lap, smiling saucily, then jumped up, and looked around her favorite table.

"Where are you hiding him, Debbie?"

"Who?"

"Lipschutz."

She wrinkled her nose and stuck out her tongue.

"You have him locked in your basement," Bingham mused. "Your love slave. Probably drugged. Sooner or later, the neighbors will notice."

Debbie pulled out a chair and sat. "Not a chance, sweetie. You spoiled me for anyone else."

"What do the Algonquins say about Lipschutz?"

"That isn't how they pronounce it."

"It is the lowest form of humor to make fun of another's name," Potts said.

"Who's the big guy with them?"

Debbie's eyes lifted. "What a dream. He used to play football. George Wintheiser."

"What are they talking about?"

"Does anyone know what Hittite is?"

"I think you wash sweaters in it."

"Well, that's what they're talking about."

"Must be a salesman. There is life after football."

"Tell it to Lipschutz."

"Let him go, Debbie. Kidnapping is a federal charge."

Debbie got up. "Anyone want dessert?"

A chorus of groans.

"Another drink?"

A chorus of happy affirmations.

4

George Wintheiser had taken to stopping by Rimini's office, although they had pretty well exhausted any topics they had in common. Hittite did not seem a promising substitute for football. George was staying through the week, at either end of which was a Notre Dame home game. He would provide color during the contests and throughout the week appear on various ESPN panels dissecting the collapse of Notre Dame football. He wanted Rimini too be a guest and an ally defending the Fighting Irish.

"If we aren't there, they will be writing our obituary."

George always sat in the easy chair, which was low, and when he crossed his legs, his huge feet seemed suspended in the air between them. Today he was wearing sneakers that were the size of snowshoes. It was the memory of those huge feet that had disturbed Rimini when he read the third news story about the Cinderella Fella.

"Those aren't Strombergs, are they?" He tried to laugh as he said it.

"Nikes." George jiggled his feet, bringing back olfactory memories of locker rooms of yore. "I do own a couple pair, however."

"Strombergs?"

George nodded. "I know what you're thinking. I read that story in the local paper. A pair of Strombergs was stolen from my motel room."

"I wouldn't tell the police that."

"Will *you?*" His smile was pleasant enough, but Rimini, in the circumstances, found it slightly menacing.

Imagine what the police would say if they asked George if he wore Strombergs and he said yes, but a pair had been stolen. Who would want shoes his size anyway?

"Have you heard anything about the effort to find out how many Catholics are on the team?"

"Did you read Bartholomew's story about the Methodist kicker and the Muslim wide receiver?"

"Interesting."

"Incredible. Admission has refused access to the press."

Rimini heard more of the same from Bartholomew Hanlon later.

"They told me all those records are confidential. Like grades. I told them about the Freedom of Information Act."

"So you're stymied?"

"Up to a point."

"You might have better luck following up on the death of Ignatius Willis."

Bartholomew ran his hand over his face. Was he trying to grow a beard? "We got a funny call. Some woman said, 'George Wintheiser wears Stromberg shoes.' "

"He does."

"How do you know that?"

"How do I know you're wearing Rockports? I can read your sole."

"Is Wintheiser still around?"

"He's staying at the Morris Inn."

That was all Rimini could do. The more he thought about it, the more it seemed that Wintheiser wanted the whistle blown on himself. It was as if he were telling Rimini: You tell them, I can't. He thought he owed it to George to let him know that *Advocata Nostra* wanted to interview him.

"They got a call telling them you wear Strombergs," he told Wintheiser.

"Was it you?"

"George. It was a woman."

"That would be Pearl."

"Your wife!"

"I wonder if it was a local call."

"Who can tell anymore?" Why would Wintheiser's wife give that kind of information to the police? "She mad at you or what?"

"Are you married?"

"A long time ago."

"Divorced?"

"Hey, I'm Catholic. No, she died."

"I'm sorry."

Rimini had felt sorry at the time; at least, he told himself he should feel sorry. How many people realized he had been married to an untamed shrew? She hated academic life and had nagged him about getting another job.

"You're an economist. There must be a lot better jobs than this."

"No doubt." No doubt. Thelma had not understood the addictive power of academic discontent. Had his griping put it into her head that he wanted out of academic life? Find me a professor who doesn't sound as if he were the lead man in a Volga boatmen crew. He suggested that she read the dialogues of Plato. She preferred Stephen King.

It was after one of their four-alarm arguments that she stormed out of the house, jumped in the car, and tore down the driveway. He heard the crash from the kitchen, where he had gone for a beer. He stood very still, refusing to think what he was thinking. He carried the still unopened bottle of beer into the living room and looked out. The street looked like a demolition derby.

Thelma had been hit first by a northbound vehicle, and that sent her spinning into the path of a southbound vehicle. Rimini had stood at the window for minutes, transfixed. The sound of their argument seemed still to be echoing in the house. A neighbor put in a call to 911. Squad cars and ambulances came screaming. There was a traffic jam for miles in either direction. Rimini waited in the house until someone rang the doorbell.

At the wake, after the funeral, he had longed to tell someone how their marriage had ended. He accepted the inarticulate condolences of friends and colleagues. He realized he was regarded as a tragic figure. Who would understand that, under a minimum of sorrow and sadness, what he really felt was relief?

Now, all these years later, he told George Wintheiser how Thelma had died.

"Right in front of your house?"

"We'd just had an argument."

The remark seemed not to register with George. But then he said, "All married people have arguments."

"You, too?"

"I may get an annulment."

"At least she remembers what brand of shoes you wear."

"Yeah. Look, I'm giving you a chance to redeem yourself."

"Redeem myself?"

"Consider what your talking to reporters stirred up. I've talked to my director at ESPN, and he likes the idea of a professor who is a former player defending the team on our channel. What do you say?"

Rimini was excited, and terrified. "Let me think about it."

"It's too late. I already said you would do it."

It helped to think it wasn't an act of free will. If he bombed, he could blame Wintheiser.

5

"First Lipschutz, now Roger," Phil said solemnly when Jimmy Stewart arrived at the Knight apartment on campus.

"You think they're connected?"

"He has an office near Roger's."

"Did you call there?"

"It's the first thing I did."

"Well, as long as it's pointless, let's go have a look."

They walked across campus. It was mottled with gold and brown leaves, but there were still many on the trees, providing a vision of loveliness that did not match Phil's mood. Going to Roger's office at least was doing something, however futile.

"No clue in the apartment?" Jimmy asked.

"None. I don't think he was there all night. I went to bed early." And feeling no pain, but Jimmy probably guessed that.

"There are faculty offices down here?" Jimmy asked as they were going down the steps beside Brownson.

"Roger prefers it."

"This has got to be one of the oldest buildings on campus."

"I'm told it was once a convent."

Jimmy said nothing to that. What was there to say?

The door was locked, but Phil used the key Roger had given him. "Just in case."

The fear went through Jimmy that this might be the case Roger had had in mind. It was with trepidation that he unlocked Roger's office. He took a deep breath and entered, flicking on the light. He went to the desk and peered over it, half fearing to find the fallen Roger lying there. But the office was empty.

"Where's Lipschutz's office?"

They went down the hall to a door that was unlocked. This office, too, was empty, but it looked messed up in a way that suggested this was not its normal condition. The wastebasket was overturned; papers had slid from their piles on the desk.

"Looks like he left in a hurry."

They went back to Roger's office to give the matter thought before they did anything else. They would have to make the rounds of everyone Roger knew, professors and students.

"Can I smoke in here?" Jimmy asked.

"Only if you light up. I'm going to call Father Carmody," Phil said. He dialed the old priest's number at Holy Cross House.

Father Carmody answered in a hearty voice.

"Father, something terrible has happened," Phil said without preamble.

"Tell me."

"It's Roger. He's disappeared."

"That would take some doing."

"Father, I'm serious. Roger's gone, and Professor Lipschutz has disappeared as well."

A slight pause. "You'd better come here so we can discuss what to do."

"I have Jimmy Stewart with me."

"Good, good. A wonderful man."

Phil hung up. "He says you're a wonderful man."

"Only my confessor knows for sure."

It was the kind of remark that reminded Phil that he was surrounded by Catholics.

Jimmy just shrugged when he said so. "You could always join the football team, Phil."

"He wants us to come to Holy Cross House."

They were outside when Phil said this. Jimmy stopped. "You mean walk?"

"We could go back to the apartment and get my car."

"That's as far as Holy Cross House."

So they walked, two middle-aged men who needed the exercise but didn't enjoy it. On this walk they were silent in order to save their breath. When Holy Cross House came in sight, Phil had a stitch in his side and Jimmy was breathing with an open mouth.

Father Carmody came to the big bowed reception desk to fetch them. The little priest was brisk, bouncy, and seemingly pleased with himself.

"Father," Phil began, but the priest held up a staying hand.

"We'll talk in my room."

Down the hall, then, where Father Carmody pushed his door open and went inside. Phil and Jimmy followed.

Roger was enthroned in the center of a sofa, a book in his hand, a beautiful view of the lake from the window he faced.

"Phil!" he cried and made a rocking motion in preparation for getting up.

"No, don't." He put a hand on Roger's shoulder and felt a great wave of tenderness go through him. That was soon followed by anger. "Have you been here all the time?"

243

"Well, since last evening."

"You didn't call! You didn't tell me where you were!"

Father Carmody intervened. "That was at my suggestion, Phil."

"Even so," Roger said. "You're a detective. I thought you would figure it out."

6

The network television crew was staying in a motel on 31, but their trucks were parked next to the stadium, where they had been throughout the season, it being more economical to just leave them there. Inside, technicians were at work and the directors confronted a huge console with a dozen or more screens. On one of them, Piero Macklin was testing field locations. He moved around as he talked, bobbing and weaving, like a boxer, like a dancer.

"Switch to Betty Boop."

This seemed to be their name for the female analyst who tossed her head, made love to the camera, and talked a mile a minute. Back to Piero then.

On one of the screens, there was an image of George Wintheiser, waiting patiently, silent. Beside him sat a nervous Professor Rimini.

"Where is he?" Jimmy asked.

"The press box."

Everything pointed to George Wintheiser. His wife, Pearl, had called to tell them her husband wore Stromberg shoes. Not an indictable offense, and Jimmy didn't want to rock the boat until he had more than the word of an obviously estranged wife. Then Larry Douglas had come in and put a plastic bag on Jimmy's desk and sat, smiling from Dumbo ear to Dumbo ear.

"What's this?"

"A present."

Jimmy looked in the bag. Shoes. Strombergs.

"Look inside them."

Jimmy looked and saw the name George Wintheiser.

"You been breaking and entering?"

"Let me tell you how I got hold of those."

Jimmy listened. He owed the kid that much at least. So it was as much dumb luck as anything that Larry had got hold of them, but nonetheless here were the shoes that matched the prints taken from the putting green and from the ground around the ball washer on the first tee. They went together, he and Larry, to the evidence room to confirm the match.

"He must have run up those stairs, down the mall, then stopped and took off his shoes and threw them in a trash barrel."

"Why would he do that?"

"We'll have to ask him."

We. Fair enough. He took Larry along when he went to have a talk with George Wintheiser. At the motel, they learned that the crew was at the stadium. Jimmy told himself that the campus was Larry's turf, he wasn't doing him any favors, but the truth was he was proud of Larry. Jimmy should have paid more attention to the story about the two women on the cleanup crew. When he dismissed them from his thoughts, it was with the notion that they couldn't tell him anything that he didn't already know.

They rose in the elevator to the top, coming out into a large reception area off which the descending levels of the press box opened. George Wintheiser was talking at the camera now. Jimmy went down to him, got his attention, and showed him his ID. The big man looked at it, nodded, and went on talking. When he was done, he swung his chair toward Jimmy.

"We found your shoes."

"How did you know they were missing?" He thought a moment. "You?" he asked the nervous bald man beside him.

"I swear to God," said Rimini.

"Tell them," Wintheiser urged.

Jimmy said, "I'd rather hear it from you."

"Someone stole a pair of my shoes. They have my name in them. You say you found them?"

"I want you to come downtown where we can talk at leisure."

"Downtown."

"To my office."

Wintheiser looked at Jimmy as if he must be kidding. "You're arresting me because someone stole my shoes?"

"No one's arresting anyone. I just want to talk."

Wintheiser thought about it. After a minute, he pressed a button and announced, "Look, I have an errand to do. Any need for me to stick around?"

A voice as if from the heavens told him he could go. He turned to Rimini. "It's up to you."

When he stood up, Jimmy saw that he was wearing shoes just like the pair Larry had brought downtown.

About an hour later, George Wintheiser decided to take the advice Jimmy had given him at the outset. First he called the network, taking down what they told him. Then he made a call to a local lawyer, Alex Cholis, who soon arrived and went into conference with his client, after which Wintheiser answered Jimmy's questions.

"A pair of shoes," Cholis said with a sad smile. Jimmy expected the lawyer to wag a disapproving finger.

"With George Wintheiser's name in them."

"They're custom made," George said.

Cholis ignored his client. "How did you come into possession of these shoes?" Jimmy had them on his desk, huge, not as shiny as the ones Wintheiser now wore, but obviously well made and expensive. Jimmy reviewed what Larry Douglas had learned.

"One of your men?"

"He's in Notre Dame campus security."

"Not one of your men."

Cholis would not have had the reputation he did if he couldn't get half an hour's diversion out of that. Had Douglas made a report? How was anyone to know whether what he had told Jimmy was true or false?

"There are the shoes," Jimmy said patiently. He liked Cholis. Everybody liked Cholis. That was how he got through your defenses.

"Indeed they are. Shoes with the name of my client in them. But what on earth significance do they have?"

Jimmy reviewed what had happened last

Sunday morning on campus: the cleaning crew, the discovery of the body of Ignatius Willis on the putting green. Cholis nodded through the recital with an approving smile, as if he might prompt Jimmy if needed.

"Very good. Very good. Now what connection is there between those shoes and the suicide found on the putting green?"

"There were footprints that match these shoes, on the green and at the first tee, where the towel from the ball washer was missing."

"The towel from the ball washer was missing," Cholis repeated with obvious delight.

His major point had been slipped in like a stiletto. The suicide on the putting green. If that was how Willis had died, they could find footprints all over the campus, they could find them on the body itself, and it would make no difference.

Jacuzzi, the prosecutor, was sitting in. He wanted to see Cholis in action. He still didn't know if they had any kind of crime here.

"The verdict of suicide is not firm."

"Either he committed suicide or he didn't. If he did, you are wasting my time and my client's."

"You know Feeney," Jacuzzi said.

"Ah."

"He thinks it might possibly have been suicide."

Cholis threw up his hands. "Gentlemen, this has been most interesting. My client and I are now going to leave." He turned and looked sadly at Jacuzzi. "Did you encourage them in this, Emile?"

The two lawyers went off down the hall, chattering away. George Wintheiser stopped in the doorway before following them.

"Can I take my shoes?"

"Not yet," Jimmy said.

He was relieved when Wintheiser left. If he had just walked over, picked up his shoes, and gone, there wouldn't have been a thing Jimmy could have done about it. It had been a miserable performance. He felt like an idiot — and he blamed Larry Douglas.

"We should have mentioned how the towel was stuffed in his mouth," Larry said.

It was because he suspected the fun Cholis could have with that that Jimmy hadn't brought it up.

"I'm going to talk to Feeney," Larry said, scrambling to his feet.

"Give him my regards."

"I have a contact in his office." Larry waited but then, getting no reaction, left.

7

When Larry stopped at his place to change into civvies, he found a note pinned to his pillow. *I love you. L.* He took the little pink square of paper and crumpled it in his fist. How in hell had she got in here? Larry wore all his keys dangling from his belt when he was in uniform. It would be like Laura to remove the key to his apartment, have a copy made, and . . . Naw. She was too dumb for that. Besides, he had other things on his mind than Laura, important things.

Thinking back over the scene in Jimmy's office, he didn't fault the detective for wanting someone to blame. And if there was anyone to blame, Larry supposed it was himself. The thing was, he remained convinced that he had done a helluva lot more than identify a pair of shoes as belonging to George Wintheiser. Cholis had made short work of Jimmy's question as to how the shoes had ended up in a trash barrel not fifty yards from where the body of Iggie Willis had been found. And Jimmy Stewart had no doubt been right not to provide Cholis more fun by mentioning how the green towel they had found was stuffed in the dead man's mouth. It didn't matter. It was Feeney's indecision that blew any case against Wintheiser out the window.

It occurred to Larry that they had never gotten around to asking what motive Wintheiser would have for killing Iggie Willis. He went back to campus and the network's command central in the huge moving-van-like truck nestled against the stadium. As he approached it, a little fellow came out the door, danced down the steps, and headed south. It was the fellow they had seen on screen before, talking from the field, Piero something.

"Hey," Larry said, running after the man. He had to yell again before the guy turned around. He waited for Larry to catch up with him.

"Do I know you?"

Larry got out his wallet and flashed it the way Jimmy had. "Police. How well do you know George Wintheiser?"

"How well? I work with the sonofabitch."

"We found his shoes, the ones that made the prints at the scene of the crime."

"No kidding."

Piero moved around on his dancer's feet, looking at Larry, waiting for more.

"The question comes up, what did Wintheiser have against Willis?"

The little guy made a face. "Talk to his wife, Pearl."

"Of course we'll do that." Jimmy had told Larry that Pearl Wintheiser had called to tell the police that her husband wore Strombergs. "Was there some kind of falling-out between them?"

Piero lit a filtered cigarette and took a deep drag, his eyes thoughtful. "I suppose there isn't anything I could tell you that you won't find out sooner or later anyway."

They went to a bench that had Moose Krause in bronze on one end and sat. More in sorrow than in anger, Piero told Larry the whole sad story. Pearl had worked for Iggie in his dental office; one thing led to another; Pearl and George broke up. "So she ends up with neither of them," Piero said. "Unless George goes back to her."

"Having taken care of the competition."

Peiro sat back, in shock. "Hey, you said that, not me."

On the way to talk to Feeney, looking ahead to seeing Kimberley there, Larry thought:

Well, we have a suspect, we have a motive. The big question is, do we have a crime? Is there a statute against stuffing a towel in a dead man's mouth?

Feeney was out, having a drink with his father, but Kimberley was there. "There's no point in waiting," she said. "It could be an hour. More."

Larry found her lovelier than ever. Once he had turned her head by whispering poetry in her ear, but Henry Grabowski had aced him out by filling that same ear with French and Latin verse. Well, he had learned a lesson from that. Larry sighed. *"Mais où sont les neiges d'antan?"*

Her eyes widened. "I thought you didn't know French."

"Not as much as I'd like to." Actually, he had only one more line and then the well was empty.

"Who wrote it?"

"Villon." His correct pronunciation was as good as another verse. Larry did not want to remember that it was Laura who had corrected him when he made the poet sound like a villain.

"What does it mean?"

"I don't suppose any translation can do justice to poetry. It really lives only in the language in which it was written."

"That's interesting." Her eyes were looking at him in the same admiring way they had before the advent of Henry.

He was about to give the line from Jules Laforgue, but he checked himself. If there was something of her former receptivity in Kimberley's manner, he didn't want to alter it by a frontal assault.

"We're still looking into the death of Ignatius Willis. Is the body still here?"

"His wife is taking her time about claiming it. It took a while to locate her. It's a darn good thing he wasn't taken away."

"Why do you say that?"

"Dr. Feeney is such a fussbudget. You know how careful he is not to give a verdict he can't back up."

"Like suicide?"

"Oh, he knows now that it couldn't have been suicide."

"He does! How?"

"He'll have to explain it to you."

By the time Feeney returned, Larry had used Jules Laforgue and a line of Latin he had found cited in an old novel. *Sed sic sic sine fine feriati.*

"Latin!" Kimberley cried. "What does it mean?"

"It's a kissing poem. 'And thus endlessly do we make holiday.' "

"Say it again. In Latin."

He did.

"What's Feeney's name doing in it?"

It might have been the coroner's cue. He came in, looked at the two young people, and kept going to his office. "I won't interrupt," he said.

But Larry followed him right into his office.

"What have you found out about the way Willis died?"

Alarm shone in Feeney's eyes. He looked accusingly at Kimberley, who had followed Larry in.

"You can't keep it a secret, Feeney."

What Feeney had found out was that someone had whacked Willis on the back of the head. This simple piece of information was woven into a fabric of excuses. He had been concentrating on the contents of the stomach, of the blood. He had found what he had found and thus had not really dwelled on the scan of the head. "He had a funny head, Larry. All kinds of unusual ridges and bumps. He was lucky he wasn't bald." When Feeney did a first cursory examination of Willis's head, he thought the welt on the back of the head was just one more oddity. "And there was no discoloration. He must have died before a bruise could form." But the blow had caused a concussion.

"Thank God," Larry cried. "Have you told Jimmy Stewart this?"

"What does it change?"

"Everything."

"So there was a concussion. Who's to say he died of that? At most it was a contributing factor."

"For God's sake, Feeney. Someone struck him down."

"His death was most likely due to alcohol poisoning."

"Would you swear to that?"

While the coroner was trying to figure out how to answer that, Larry picked up Feeney's phone and called Jimmy Stewart. Feeney looked on in alarm as Larry said, "Stewart, Feeney has just told me that Willis was struck on the back of the head. Causing a concussion. That means he was attacked!"

Larry noticed that Kimberley was admiring his decisive manner.

"I'll be right over," Jimmy said.

"I'll be here."

8

When Roger had brought the unraveled Lipschutz to Holy Cross House, his usually condescending colleague had been reduced to a whimpering whining parody of his usual imperious self. He had been publicly humiliated, he had been physically threatened. Was it possible that a full professor could be treated in this way? Roger made soothing remarks as they whisked along the lake path and then climbed slowly up a steep incline to the level of Holy Cross House. The entrance on the lake side of the retirement home was close to Father Carmody's room. Lights were on in the old priest's apartment. Leaving the cowering Lipschutz in the golf cart, Roger went and tapped on Father Carmody's window. He could see the old priest respond to the noise, but he seemed not to know where it was coming from. The next time, Roger tapped on his window with his keys. In response, the window went dark. Roger stepped back and waved his arms. Only with the light out could Father Carmody see him.

The window cranked open. "Roger?"

"Could you let us in, Father?"

"I'll come to the door on this side of the house. Do you know where it is?"

"Yes, Father."

Roger went back to his golf cart and parked it closer to the entrance, which was soon opened.

"Come," Roger said, getting a hand under Lipschutz's elbow. Lipschutz was docile still, and Roger guided him to the door and inside. At the sight of Father Carmody, Lipschutz let out an anguished cry.

"You!" Face-to-face with the agent of his public humiliation, Lipschutz began to tremble. He turned as if to go. Father Carmody got hold of Lipschutz's other arm, and they steered him into the old priest's room.

"What's wrong with him?"

"He's had several unnerving experiences."

"You tore up my petition," Lipschutz said accusingly.

"Kindest thing I could have done for you."

"I can't stay here. This is impossible."

They got him into a chair, and Father Carmody called for a nurse. She came and listened and probed. "I don't see anything wrong with him. I'll call the doctor."

"No need for that, my dear. What this man needs is rest. A sedative."

In that house, this was equivalent to little more than an aspirin. The nurse went off on her squeaky shoes and was soon back with some tablets in a little paper cup.

"What is that?" Lipschutz's eyes rolled from the nurse to Roger and then fleetingly to his nemesis, Father Carmody.

"Just something to relax you," Roger promised.

Relax him it did. Before he went completely under, the nurse led him off to an empty room, in which Lipschutz would enjoy some fifteen hours of uninterrupted sleep. Meanwhile, Roger dined with Father Carmody in the refectory, the inhabitants who could get about settled at tables all around them. In this company, Father Carmody looked almost young. Afterward, back in Father Carmody's room, they reviewed the events of the past week. Roger had talked to Phil some hours before and was able to describe the finding of the Stromberg shoes and the questioning of George Wintheiser.

"George Wintheiser! The football player? Impossible."

■ ■ ■ ■

The necessary is what cannot not be, the possible what can be, and what better sign that something can be than that it actually is? In other moods, on other topics, Father Carmody might have appreciated Roger's metaphysical reminders, but in the case of George Wintheiser he was in the classical position of the confidante, or in this case confessor, who knows more than he can say. He had meant it when he declared it impossible that George Wintheiser should be involved in the death of Iggie Willis. On the other hand, he knew of the reckless liaison between Iggie and George's wife, the irrepressible Pearl. This had led to her alienation from George, separation, talk of annulment and divorce, and the separation of Iggie and his wife. Two impossible women. No possible. After all, as Roger had reminded him, what is actual is possible. *Ab esse ad posse valet illatio.*

Father Carmody was not a misogynist. He knew many admirable women. His devotion to the Blessed Virgin, the patron of the university, was deep and heartfelt. Years ago, though, when George had introduced him to Pearl, Father Carmody had felt forebodings. He remembered an old song, too old for George to know: "You can bring Pearl, she's a darn nice girl, but don't bring Lulu. . . . I'll bring her myself." Pearl was a lovely young girl, a St. Mary's girl, talking, laughing, clinging to George's arm; why hadn't he been able to see them as just another happy young couple? To say that Pearl had the eyes of a cat would only reveal that Father Carmody had never liked cats. Possessive as Pearl was of George, she seemed always to be flirting, looking around . . .

All of this was pure speculation, of course, and Father Carmody would not for the life of him have said any of it aloud. Still, such thoughts had lessened the delight he felt when he presided over the wedding of Pearl and George, transforming them into Mr. and Mrs. George Wintheiser. If Pearl seemed too flighty and immature to be a bride, George seemed miscast as a football player. He *was* a great football player, at Notre Dame and later with Green Bay, but professor after professor had told Father Carmody that the huge young man was one of the best students they had ever had. Of course, there is no contradiction between brain and brawn, no matter what Aristotle said. How many could acquire a doctorate almost in their spare time, let alone a doctorate in Hittite? George had no desire to become an academic, however, and dismissed Father Carmody's suggestion that he become Notre Dame's designated Hittite.

"Study's for fun, Father. Sports is my work."

But of course sports turns one into a nomad, first as a player, later, in George's case, as a commentator, flying around the country from game to game. Not an ideal background for a marriage. Not when one had a wife like Pearl and there were such chuckleheads in the world as Iggie Willis. Father Carmody had not been surprised when George came to tell him it was all over between him and Pearl.

"What do you think of annulments, Father?"

"Don't get me started."

"You don't approve of them?"

Careful, careful. Father Carmody did not aspire to be more Catholic than the Church. It wasn't annulments, per se, as he once would have said, but the way they were being dished out that caused dismay. Catholic divorce, as cynics said. Not even God can make what has been not to have been. An annulment was the judgment that a marriage had not taken place, that there was nothing to dissolve. Having presided at the Wintheiser wedding, Father Carmody was not inclined to think it hadn't happened. Flawed acts, acts that are later regretted, remain acts that did happen.

Enough. Roger Knight was a bad influence on him. The next thing he knew he would be discoursing on the real distinction between essence and existence. Meanwhile, he went downtown to be with George in this difficult hour.

9

The second interrogation of George Wintheiser led to his arraignment and incarceration. "Incarceration" was the word that Cholis, his wily lawyer, used each time he referred to his client's confinement in the county jail, under suspicion of wrongful contribution to the death of another. His pronunciation of the word involved a series of exaggerated facial expressions, each of which he held for perhaps a beat longer than necessary. So said, the word conjured up the prisoner of Zenda, the poor little shoemaker from *A Tale of Two Cities,* and other victims of injustice. Cholis explicitly alluded to St. Paul and the Roman prison. "In that case, as in this, the angel of truth will lead an innocent man forth from captivity." Indeed, it was not long before Cholis had Wintheiser out on bail.

"I didn't do it, Father," Wintheiser said when, having stooped to avoid hitting his head, he came into the visiting room where Father Carmody awaited him. Then he realized the priest was not alone.

"Have you met Roger Knight, George?"

"I have." The two men shook hands, contrasting specimens of the species. George could have been the model for Michelangelo's David, whereas Roger . . . Well, there was a lot to Roger, but it wasn't distributed in a way that would interest a sculptor. Both men had difficulty getting comfortable on the chairs in the visiting room.

"I didn't do it, Father."

Father Carmody looked him in the eye. "I know that. The problem is that we have to prove it. It is said a negative cannot be proved. If that were so, the whole criminal court system is reared on a fallacy. Where were you when whatever happened to Iggie happened?"

"Early last Sunday morning? I went to six o'clock Mass in the lower basilica."

"Six!" Even the old priest was surprised.

Wintheiser turned to Roger. "Do you know Greg Walsh, in the university archives?"

"Know him? He's a friend of mine."

"He's become a friend of mine. Not everyone you run into knows much about the ancient languages of the Middle East.

In my spare moments, I've been visiting the archives. Stolen moments. Greg offered to let me in early Sunday. That would give me hours before I had to go on television."

"And you spent those hours in the archives in the library."

"From about seven until eleven thirty."

"And before all that? Before the six o'clock Mass."

"My motel. I went to bed fairly early, well, before midnight. I asked to be called at five fifteen."

"Have you told the police this?" Roger asked.

"They're checking it out."

"Trying to disprove an affirmative?"

Wake-up calls at the motel, it turned out, were computerized. When a guest asked to be called at a particular time, it was entered along with the room number, and at that time the phone in the room in question rang. After seven rings, the phone shut itself off, but if no one in the room responded to the first call, another was made ten minutes later. The difficulty lay in the fact that there was no record of that second call having been answered or not.

"There was a second call?"

"I never heard the first."

"Can anyone confirm all this?"

268

George glanced at Roger, then leaned toward Father Carmody. "Pearl."

"Pearl!"

"We're still married, Father."

Father Carmody lifted his hands as if to forestall any details on the marital state. Pearl, George's estranged wife, had shown up unannounced and called him from the lobby, and he told her to come on up.

"The place was full. She would have had to sleep in the lobby."

"What time did she arrive?"

"Everyone asks me that. I didn't even turn on the light. I propped the door open and got back into bed."

"And Pearl came up?"

"Yes."

Again they were on the edge of matters as mysterious and unintelligible to Roger as to the old celibate. The thought that occurred to Father Carmody he did not voice until he and Roger were headed back to campus.

"Pearl had as much motive to put an end to Iggie Willis as George. And think of it, she was here."

Roger hummed for a moment. "What size shoe does she wear?"

10

Guido Senzamacula peeked around his half-opened door and, seeing Lipschutz, tried to close it again, but his colleague's shoe seemed a practiced door stopper.

"Guido, we must talk."

"No! You are a traitor. I did not sign your statement."

"Of course you didn't."

Silence on the other side of the door; then Guido peeked out at him again. "You admit that?"

"I admit that."

The door swung open. Although it was midafternoon, Guido wore pajamas. There were little drying puffs of shaving cream beneath his earlobes.

"You must write that down. You must promise to explain it to my son."

His son! Lipschutz managed not to shiver. A bonus of what he was about would be the comeuppance of that young thug. "Yes, yes.

Anything you wish. Do I smell coffee?"

"I am not an authority on your sense data." A great smile broke out on Guido's face. It was the first thing he had said in character for longer than he cared to think.

"That's true."

Lipschutz followed Guido into the kitchen, where indeed there was coffee. Reheated coffee, as it happened. Yesterday's coffee. Perhaps worse. They sat at the kitchen table.

"With the nonsense of the petition out of the way, we can turn our minds to important things. Let them play football, Guido, I don't care. Let them play football all year long, it is all right with Horst Lipschutz. But the work of the university, its true work, must go on, and that, Guido, is up to us."

"Then God help the university."

"Help will be needed. Yes. Very large sums if my calculations are correct, but with you as the proposed director of the center . . ."

"Me! What are you talking about?"

Lipschutz adopted a knowing look. "Guido, like it or not, we live in a football culture. We must take that into account. You mentioned your son."

"Piero?"

"Piero. A young man who is well known because of his work broadcasting Notre

Dame football games."

"He is a good boy."

"With many contacts, I'm sure."

"You mean benefactors?"

No need to spell everything out now. "This is very interesting coffee."

"Do you find it too hot?"

Not hot enough. But could anything conceal the taste?

Il faut d'abord durer. The maxim was almost Darwinian. First, one must survive — and Lipschutz was a survivor. The traumatic events of recent days had been put into perspective. When he awoke from his fifteen hours of drug-induced sleep in Holy Cross House, he had risen like the son of the widow of Naim to a new life. Past mistakes must be acknowledged, but not brooded over. They were important only insofar as they suggested future action. Lipschutz had been gracious to Father Carmody, grateful for his hospitality, no allusion whatsoever to the contretemps on the steps of the Main Building. Don't get mad, get even. Withdraw and regroup.

Roger was gone; Lipschutz said he would walk to campus. He went down the path to the lake. A first ice had formed, hardly thick enough to warrant taking a shortcut across the lake. He imagined himself in a scene from *Uncle Tom's Cabin,* Eliza escaping, leaping from ice floe to ice floe. That such a book should have hastened a country into civil war seemed a testimonial to the power of ideas and imagination, even defective ones.

The Center for Advanced Studies would be built — perhaps there was still some virgin littoral stretch and the building he envisaged could be nestled somewhere along this lake or the other — but there were to be modifications in the plan. Was it his realization that the Father Carmody who had publicly humiliated him had no known position in the administration, yet was a powerful man? An authority next to which titular authority paled to insignificance? Lipschutz had a moment of candor, of self-knowledge. "I am not well liked," Lipschutz told himself. "I am not liked at all. At best I am admired, but even that is grudging. There are some, I am told, who find me a comic character. Horst Lipschutz, a comic character! That is indeed comic." There was no need for him to endorse these judgments of himself, but he could not ignore them, no matter the unfavorable light it cast on those who made them. The center needed a front man, a likable man, a man everyone felt comfortable with. So he had gone to knock on Guido Senzamacula's door, running the risk of encountering that maniac of a son who had nearly shaken the life out of him. Guido had that spontaneous emotional nature, gushing forth whatever came to mind, irresistible, and to that Italian, that Mediterranean, charm, Guido had added the patina of smoothness derived from the French. The world could be divided into those who wish they were Italian and those who wish they were French. The twain had met in Guido. He would be a perfect figurehead.

Some hours later, after a few phone calls, Lipschutz was on his way to the Morris Inn to have a drink with the reputedly filthy rich Mimi O'Toole.

11

In the next room, Roger and Father Carmody were talking just loudly enough to
make it difficult for Phil to follow the
nonsense he was hearing on ESPN. With
George Wintheiser out of the picture, it was
open season on the Irish and no defenders
on the scene except Professor Rimini, bald
as an egg, a kind of six-cylinder Dick Vitale.
He was better than nothing, but what isn't?

"Ty was bounced for doing better than
this," the ineffable Kornheiser cried.
"Where's the fairness, where's the equity?"

Who put that idiot in charge of the uni-
verse? And NBC had brought back the
smug Olbermann on Sunday nights, another
know-it-all, and a Clinton shill besides.
What next, Dan Rather at the Daytona 500?
Maybe there *was* a conspiracy. Could Charlie Weis be a mole of the forces of evil?

Phil pressed the mute button and put back
his head. The voices from the next room

were almost soothing.

"Work out the time line, Roger. She shows up at his motel when?"

"It's pretty vague."

"It's precise enough to make one wonder what she was doing up till then."

"I suppose the police could establish that."

"Roger, she left home a week ago. Where has she been? What has she been doing?"

Phil rolled out of his beanbag chair and joined them. "And if anyone had a reason to bonk Iggie Willis, she did."

A woman used and cast aside, a woman spurned. A woman who had turned from the Hyperion George to the satyr Iggie. A woman who had tapped on George's door in the wee hours of last Sunday morning and been admitted on the basis of vows that last a lifetime.

"Before the reconciliation, she had to clear the decks."

"Slay the satyr."

"No more reminder of her infidelity."

"Phil," Roger cried. "You've become a poet."

Father Carmody was not to be dissuaded. Did he really think that the death of Iggie could be traced to Pearl? It didn't matter whether he thought that or not. What one needed was something Cholis the magnificent could use to sow doubt in the minds of twelve good men and true.

"That's a relief," Roger said. "You can't expect them to take action against Pearl Wintheiser."

"I couldn't imagine them accusing George," the old priest said, almost petulantly.

12

Death camp commandants have wept while listening to Mozart; serial killers are described by the neighbors as good and thoughtful boys. The inner is not the outer; human beings are mysterious mixtures of good and bad.

Having thought such thoughts in solitude, Roger voiced them to Greg Walsh. The associate archivist nodded. The subject was George Wintheiser, who was being held in connection with the death of Iggie Willis. It was the fact that Iggie had an affair with Pearl, George's wife, that sustained the accusation. Roger remembered the way in which the huge former football player had plied Iggie with drink at their party after the game. The fact that Iggie had reeled from their apartment in the wee hours of the morning and staggered across campus to, of all places, Rockne Memorial, there to be attacked, made Roger feel almost responsible for the dentist's tragic end.

"George came to the archives often?"

"Well, he had been here before. On football weekends."

Could a man whose doctorate was in Middle Eastern languages with a concentration in Hittite kill his wife's former lover?

Could a mass murderer love Mozart?

On the face of it, the questions were silly, but it is the silly questions we pursue most doggedly.

"He was here in the archives the Sunday morning after the Boston College game?"

Greg Walsh, no more than Roger, measured time according to the schedule of the football team, but he understood.

"Yes, he was here. The monitor let him in so he could take the elevator up here."

The two men were talking in the archives on the sixth floor of the Hesburgh Library, in Greg's office.

"Of course. The library opens late on Sundays."

Still, an early Sunday morning visit to the archives, like knowledge of Hittite, did not rule George Wintheiser out as Iggie Willis's assailant.

"What did he come here to see? Have you anything of interest to a man with his scholarly specialty?"

"Oh, he wanted to look at old issues of the *Scholastic.*"

"He did?" That the cultivated former football player should have arisen at dawn one Sunday morning in order to go to an early Mass and then come on to the archives to pore over old issues of what had once been the chief student publication was a disappointment. "You'll have a record of what he wanted to look at?"

"Of course."

Greg consulted his records, and soon the relevant bound volumes of the *Scholastic* were on the table before them. Roger would not presume on their friendship and ask Greg to engage in the doubtless absurd effort of going through those volumes. Soon he was alone in the room, slowly turning the glossy pages of issues that dated back to George Wintheiser's student days.

Apart from articles devoted to sports, George did not appear in the issues that Roger went through, page by page, trying not to think of Sisyphus rolling a huge rock up a mountain. Ignatius Willis, by contrast, popped up again and again, an officer of his class from sophomore year on, chairman of dance committees, apparently stellar student as well. President of the French Club. Roger leaned over the page to study a photograph.

Professor Guido Senzamacula smiled back at him from decades ago, flanked by his star students. The student on his right, Ignatius Willis, was only a head taller than the professor, but the boy on his left, runner-up for the medal Senzamacula was about to present, towered over him. George Wintheiser.

Guido Senzamacula was delighted to see Roger but surprised at the reason for his visit.

"Is the Chateaubriand Medal still awarded by your department?"

Guido threw up his hands. "The Chateubriand Medal! I had forgotten all about that. Will you have some wine?"

"No, no thanks."

"Espresso, then?"

Espresso would be fine. When Guido returned with a tray on which were two diminutive cups and a large bowl of sugar, Roger was settled on the middle cushion of the couch. Guido was shaking his head. "The Chateaubriand Medal."

"The medal once won by Ignatius Willis."

Having seated himself and sipped his coffee, Guido sighed. "The last recipient."

"The last!"

"It is a painful story."

Wherever there are contests, there is the temptation to win by any means. Wherever there are rankings, there is the danger of misapplying criteria for base motives. Wherever there are prizes and medals, it is they rather than the performance they are meant to certify that is sought. Ignatius Willis had been awarded the Chateaubriand Medal on the basis of a plagiarized essay. That it was plagiarized was brought to the knowledge of the committee by an anonymous note. Guido alone of the committee members thought even an anonymous accusation should be disposed of. It was he who learned that the accusation was just.

"The medal was revoked?"

"Oh, no. I was outvoted. It would have been too great a scandal."

It was an almost pleasant thought that once a plagiarized paper on Chateaubriand's visit to President Washington in Philadelphia could loom so large as a threat to the reputation of a school.

"Father Carmody was very persuasive. I very nearly changed my own vote after listening to him."

"George Wintheiser should have won the medal?"

"The next boy, yes, the runner-up. He had been my choice." Guido smiled. "I was outvoted so often in those days."

"Do you remember Wintheiser's topic?"

Guido put back his head and closed his eyes, humming as if to give his memory the proper pitch. His head snapped down. "Peguy's long poem on Chartres."

"By a football player!"

"Oh, he was a brilliant student, no doubt of that."

"Did he know he had been cheated out of the medal?"

"Good heavens, no. Only the committee knew. The one thing we agreed on was that the medal had been tainted. We decided not to award it again."

"But Ignatius Willis knew you knew."

"I confronted him, Roger."

"And?"

Guido waved his hand, dismissing the topic. "It was all a long time ago."

Father Carmody was reluctant to discuss the matter of the Chateaubriand Medal.

"Anicent history, Roger. Ancient history."

"I have spoken to Professor Senzamacula."

"Wonderful man. A man of great integrity."

"He was outvoted on the matter of revoking the medal."

"That was my doing." Father Carmody

puffed thoughtfully on his cigarette. "Ah, the sins of one's past life."

"You regret persuading the committee to keep the plagiarism quiet?"

"Yes and no."

"You half regret it?"

"The idiot who won the medal by cheating was confronted by Senzamacula."

"So he told me."

"Did he tell you the rest?"

"What was the rest?"

Suddenly the gentle professor of French was the object of a campaign to make him look like a bumbling fool. Jokes in the *Scholastic*, things written on the board of his classroom, practical jokes.

"It was the water bomb that undid him."

Apparently dropped from a third-floor window of O'Shaughnessy, the water bomb had exploded at Senzamacula's feet.

"He had lost his son, a poor retarded little fellow they loved as parents do love such a child, and his wife was already gone. Now this campaign to make him look foolish. He had a nervous breakdown."

"Who was behind all this?"

"Your guess is as good as mine." He stubbed out his cigarette. "Your guess is probably the same as mine."

"But nothing was done?"

284

"Let sleeping dogs lie."

Roger directed his golf cart back to his office in Brownson. What is more conducive to thought than a silent battery-run vehicle that seems to know where you want it to go? He parked in the lot next to the old building and looked up at the spire of Sacred Heart just visible over the hulk of the basilica. As he eased himself from behind the wheel, there was the sound of a car door closing. He turned to see a spry, familiar little fellow approaching.

"Professor Knight?"

Piero put out his hand, and Roger took it. "Yes."

"Could we talk?"

"In my office."

Roger led the way inside and down the corridor to his door, which he unlocked and entered, Piero following, As he eased himself into his commodious chair, he heard the sound of the door lock being turned. Piero took a chair across from Roger's desk.

"You've been talking with my father."

The thoughts he had been trying to sort out on his way from Holy Cross House became suddenly clear, pieces of a puzzle fitting together.

"Yes."

"He never really recovered from that harassment, you know. And when my brother died, he had a relapse. He would have retired if it hadn't been for Father Carmody's persuasion."

"He is one of my dearest colleagues."

"Father Carmody?"

"Your father."

Roger was remembering how Piero had assaulted poor Horst. Had he been a surrogate for Ignatius Willis, a reminder of the campaign against Guido that had driven the gentle professor into a nervous breakdown?

"What size shoe do you wear, Piero?"

The young man sat back in his chair, his expression sad. He nodded. "So you have figured it out."

■ ■ ■ ■

PART FOUR

■ ■ ■ ■

1

Phil and Jimmy Stewart were having a late lunch in Legends, the restaurant immediately south of the stadium.

"Cholis will get him off," Jimmy said.

"Everything points to him."

"Yes."

That bothered Jimmy. It bothered Phil, too. Talking with Pearl Wintheiser hadn't helped. She reminded Jimmy of his flown wife; she reminded Phil of several women he was glad he hadn't married. Her clothes would have been appropriate for a younger woman; her eyes were made up in a glittering way, green eyelids, spiky lashes. It was clear that she wanted them to notice that she was a woman, as she clearly noticed that they were men. She laughed when Jimmy asked if she had spent last Saturday night in her husband's motel room.

"Why would you think that?"

"Someone mentioned it."

"George?" Then, theatrically, she understood. "I'm his alibi?"

"Were you in the motel that night?"

She dipped her chin. "I don't have to answer that."

"Of course not."

She looked sultry. "I was in the Morris Inn."

"So was Iggie Willis."

"Not that night! He never showed up."

"And now we know why."

Jimmy said to Roger, "I don't think Cholis will put her on the stand."

"No, but Jacuzzi will."

If George Wintheiser had lied about his wife coming to his motel room that night, it could have been because he knew that she had gone to Iggie's room in the Morris Inn.

They were still there when Larry Douglas came in, wearing his uniform as a member of campus security. Laura was with him, her bulk putting a severe strain on her uniform.

"Can we join you?" Larry asked.

"Take a pew."

Laura splayed her left hand on the table; she waved it in front of her face; she laid it again on the table. Ah, the ring. All eyes dropped to it. Larry looked at Jimmy and Phil like a condemned man.

"Congratulations," Jimmy said.

"It is the man you congratulate," Laura said coyly.

The way you give a condemned man a hearty last meal. Poor Larry.

"You've been a lot of help, Larry," Jimmy told him.

"I've got to get on the South Bend police force."

"You do not!" Laura said. "That's too dangerous."

Phil got out his cell phone and called the apartment. No answer. He called Roger's office. No answer there either.

"Oh, he's in his office," Larry said. "At least he was a few minutes ago."

"How do you know?"

"His golf cart was in the lot."

Phil rose and bade the others good-bye. In his car, he started for the apartment. Roger must be in transit. But Roger was not at home. Phil did not get out of the car but headed toward Brownson. The golf cart was in the parking lot.

The outer door was unlocked, but when he got to Roger's office his knock was unanswered. For years he had been looking out for his precocious younger brother, protecting him, a surrogate parent. He lowered his shoulder and crashed into the door, splintering it. He stumbled into the office.

"Phil," Roger said.

A man had leaped up from the chair and absurdly assumed a karate stance.

"This is Professor Senzamacula's son. He wears a size seven and a half shoe."

Piero sprang at Phil, uttering a great cry. Phil grabbed his arm, turned, and decided not to flip him over his shoulder. Instead, he drove a fist into his midsection. Piero went down with a groan.

■ ■ ■ ■

EPILOGUE

■ ■ ■ ■

Winter came with spring not far behind, and on the practice field players and coaches began to prepare for the coming football season. Hope springs eternal. Philip Knight and Jimmy Stewart were on the sidelines, in Roger's golf cart, looking on.

"They can't possibly be as bad as last year," Jimmy said.

"That is our prayer."

Prayer was not forgotten. Provisions were made for pauses in practice so that John Foster Natashi and his coreligionists could spread their little rugs and pray to Allah. John Wesley was agitating for a Methodist minister to attend to the spiritual needs of himself and others of like persuasion. Campus ministry was enthusiastic.

A large man in a tweed jacket and turtle-neck, a Notre Dame cap on his head, came toward them.

"How are you, George?"

Wintheiser opened his hands. "The question is, how are they?"

The team. Wintheiser had come through the ordeal of last fall well. According to Father Carmody, he was reunited with Pearl. No comment, just a statement. Till death do us part. The old priest was urging that George be awarded the Chateaubriand Medal, however belatedly. Neil Genoux was interested. It seemed a small step toward reconciling disenchanted alumni with their alma mater. Answers to the inquiries of the Weeping Willow Society had gone out that, while their obliquity would have been the envy of any diplomat, nonetheless acknowledged the society's existence. It was hard for Phil not to notice George's shoes as he walked away.

The dismissal of charges against George Wintheiser had of course been inevitable when a suddenly repentant Piero Macklin told all. His confession was so heartfelt that Alex Cholis was happy to take his case.

"Filial love," he purred, doubtless thinking of what he could do with that in court.

The phrase seemed an accurate enough description of what had triggered such wrath in the television director. His father's reaction to having his name appear on Lipschutz's list, the mocking of the signatories, had brought back the long-ago attacks on his father that had led to a nervous breakdown, and now here was the culprit, Ignatius Willis, rallying alumni in his attack on the football team. Something snapped in that noble breast, as Cholis would doubtless put it. But why had he stolen a pair of Wintheiser's size fourteen Strombergs and worn them over his own shoes when he stalked Iggie and laid him low on the putting green next to Rockne Memorial? It seemed that he had thought Wintheiser's defense of the Fighting Irish during their 2007 collapse could have been more forceful, although surely nobody else had thought so. Cholis dismissed the problem.

"You mustn't seek a rational motive in a man so intent on avenging his father against the man who had mocked him."

Piero, saddened by the outcome of the game but gripped by melancholy, was just setting off for a moonlit tour of campus when he saw George drop Iggie off at the Morris Inn. Piero intercepted the weaving Willis and led him right through the inn, through the tent in back, and onto the putting green.

"Why?"

"He needed air. So did I."

It was Iggie's drunken mockery of the Lipschutz group that altered the character of their midnight stroll. Iggie promised to post their names and photographs on his Web site and invite alumni to let them know what they thought of the idea of abandoning football. That brought back memories too bitter to withstand.

The matter of the towel from the golf ball washer on the first tee never came up in the trial. Piero confided in Father Carmody his reason for stuffing it in the mouth of the man he had just struck down. It seemed that Willis had not only been a plagiarizer, he cheated at golf, once depriving Piero of a prize for the least number of putts in an alumni tournament.

"Did you think you had killed him?"

"Father, I took one swing at him and that was that. I thought I had just knocked him out."

"Does your lawyer know that?"

"I've told him everything."

"I wouldn't want to be on that jury," Roger said to Father Carmody.

"I just hope he doesn't connect his defense too closely to the university."

A wan hope, that, but a tribute to Father

Carmody's unswerving loyalty to Notre Dame.

Mimi O'Toole, to the dismay of the administration, had been moved by Lipschutz's vision of a research center. After a talk with Frank Parkman, she had persuaded her husband to put up the money for it. It was Mimi, Lipschutz explained to Guido Senzamacula, who had insisted that he, Horst Lipschutz, be the director. Now the administration was looking around for a building to tear down so the center could be built.

One April afternoon, sitting in the sun on the lakeside of Holy Cross House, Father Carmody asked Roger what he was teaching this semester.

"Do you know William Butler Yeats, Father?"

"Tell me about him."

Roger did, highlighting the poet's two visits to Notre Dame.

"An Irishman?"

"Yes."

"Catholic?"

"Oh, no. Anglo-Irish."

A nonecumenical remark seemed about to be made, but Father Carmody held his tongue. He listened with feigned interest as

Roger recited "The Second Coming."

" 'Slouching towards Bethlehem to be born?' "

Roger let it go. Turning poetry into prose is seldom a satisfying exercise.

"He was a great admirer of the then president, Father O'Donnell. The priest poet of Notre Dame."

"Good man."

Did Father Carmody mean O'Donnell or Yeats? Roger decided not to ask.

ABOUT THE AUTHOR

Ralph McInerny is the author of more than forty books, including the popular Father Dowling series, and has taught for over fifty years at the University of Notre Dame, where he is the director of the Jacques Maritain Center. He has been awarded the Bouchercon Lifetime Achievement Award and was appointed to the President's Committee on the Arts and Humanities. He lives in South Bend, Indiana.